Pricilla st...
appeared ...

Without he... ...as forced to squint. She fumbled for her glasses, slid them on, and then turned back to the window. Two figures struggled in the moonlight, but she couldn't make out the details. Dark clothing. . .a flash of metal. . .glasses on the larger figure. . .

She shuddered.

The lifeless body of Reggie Pierce filled her mind, but she shoved it away. Reggie, and Charles Woodruff for that matter, were completely different situations. Stumbling across a murdered victim twice in her life was bad enough. Three times. . .

Other mysteries by Lisa Harris

Recipe for Murder
Baker's Fatal Dozen

Don't miss out on any of our great mysteries. Contact us at the
following address for information on our newest releases and club
information:

Heartsong Presents—MYSTERIES! Readers' Service
PO Box 721
Uhrichsville, OH 44683
Web site: www.heartsongmysteries.com

Or for faster action, call 1-740-922-7280.

Chef's Deadly Dish

A Cozy Crumb Mystery

Lisa Harris

HEARTSONG
PRESENTS
MYSTERIES

ISBN 978-1-60260-305-9

Scripture taken from the HOLY BIBLE, NEW INTERNATIONAL
VERSION®. NIV®. Copyright © 1973, 1978, 1984 by International
Bible Society. Used by permission of Zondervan. All rights reserved.

All of the characters and events in this book are fictitious. Any
resemblance to actual persons, living or dead, or to actual events is
purely coincidental.

Cover design: Kirk DouPonce, DogEared Design
Cover illustration: Jody Williams

*Our mission is to publish and distribute inspirational products offering
exceptional value and biblical encouragement to the masses.*

Printed in the United States of America.

1

The fact that she'd already seen the wedding dress didn't stop Pricilla Crumb's jaw from dropping. She searched for a word of encouragement to give her future daughter-in-law, but none surfaced at the sight of the satin gown hanging like a shapeless gunnysack on Trisha Summers's slender frame.

Lord, this is one of those days when an extra miracle would be greatly appreciated.

Pricilla paced the carpeted floor of suite twenty-three in the Silvermist Lodge and shook her head. With the wedding only three weeks away, the express package had arrived not only late but two sizes too big. Yards of satin swallowed Trisha in their creamy swirls, while the puffy sleeves jutted to the side like oversized football pads.

Trisha blinked back the tears and sniffled as she looked down at Riley Michaels, who'd been called in to help salvage the gown. "It's hopeless, isn't it?"

"Fiddlesticks," Riley spoke through a mouthful of pins. "Nothing's hopeless."

Pricilla moved to hand Trisha another tissue. "If anyone can save your dress, Riley can. She comes highly recommended."

"Thank you, Mrs. Crumb. And she's right, Trisha. You don't need to worry one bit." Riley's brow puckered as she knelt to examine the lace hem, her stoic expression far less encouraging than her words. "Give me a few days, and we'll have this dress looking as if it were made for you."

"Didn't I tell you everything would be all right,

Trisha?" Pricilla worked to add some enthusiasm to her words, but she'd never understand the compulsion to buy things off the Internet. And a wedding dress of all things. Even if it was exactly what Trisha had been looking for, the oversized gown simply proved Pricilla's theory that shopping via the World Wide Web was a modern pitfall to be avoided. "I was told you won't find a better seamstress than Riley anywhere around, and from what I've seen so far, I can see why."

"I'm sure you're right." Trisha blew her nose. "But if I didn't know better, I'd say this wedding was jinxed."

"What else has gone wrong?" Riley pulled a pin from her mouth and eased it into the fabric.

Fresh tears brimmed in Trisha's eyes. "For starters, our invitations were printed *Nathan and Janet*, instead of *Nathan and Trisha*."

Half a dozen pins spewed to the floor as Riley burst out laughing. She clasped her hand against her mouth and began picking up the scattered pins. "I'm sorry. They fixed the problem, didn't they?"

"They replaced the invitations, but not the days of stress I had to endure as a result." Trisha wrinkled her reddened nose. "All I have to say is a week's honeymoon in the Bahamas with Nathan can't come soon enough. I'm beginning to dread my own wedding."

"He did get the engagement ring right," Riley said. "It's absolutely stunning."

Trisha smiled for the first time. "It is gorgeous, isn't it? Nathan had it specially made with a stone he got in South Africa when he was there on a hunting trip a few years ago."

"That is so romantic."

While she certainly didn't believe in jinxes, Pricilla had to admit Trisha had a point. With the wedding ceremony around the corner, it seemed that the planning of the blessed event had taken a nosedive and gone completely off course. She'd suggested hiring a wedding coordinator, but Trisha insisted she wanted the experience of planning the event herself. As much as she loved the girl, Pricilla wished she could find a way to knock some sense into her.

"Have you ever thought about eloping?" Riley shoved a lock of her short red hair behind her ear, barely missing a beat as she continued marking the alterations with another pin.

The question produced a pair of raised brows from Trisha, but Pricilla thought the woman had a legitimate point. She glanced down at the simple diamond engagement ring on her own finger and wondered about her upcoming nuptials. The word *elope* had entered into a number of conversations with her fiancé, Max, in hushed tones. Despite the scandalous feel the idea rendered, if the truth be told, it was sounding more and more like a good idea. She didn't need a fancy dress, dozens of guests, and piles of rich food as an essential backdrop for her to proclaim her love to Max. A wedding ring on her finger and a marriage certificate from the court would be enough for her.

Pricilla pulled a complimentary issue of *Food Style* magazine off the coffee table as Trisha jumped into a monologue about why she was insisting on a genuine old-fashioned wedding. But a peek at the magazine only managed to exchange one stressful encounter for another. The glossy photograph of filet mignon and browned-to-perfection potatoes served as a reminder that a substitute chef now stood in Pricilla's kitchen at the Rendezvous Hunting Lodge and Resort. While she looked forward to her role as emcee for the renowned Rocky Mountain Chef Competition, even her son Nathan's repeated assurances that all would be fine under the strict eye of her weekend replacement had done little to erase her apprehensions.

"Have you and Max set a date yet?"

Pricilla's chin tipped up when she realized that Riley was addressing her. "Max and I? Not yet." She glanced back at Trisha. "I believe I have enough to worry about at the moment. I am the mother of the groom, you know."

And her son had always come first.

Riley cocked her head. "I've always believed that there's no use putting off a good thing."

Pricilla flipped the page. At sixty-five, she hadn't expected Prince Charming to come waltzing into her life, but Max Summers, friend of nearly four decades, had indeed swept in and stolen her heart in the process. While she planned to say "I do" before their children considered sending them to a retirement center, two weddings were simply too much to plan at the same time. Especially with all the complications encountered with this one.

Riley stuck in another pin. "How much time do I have?"

Pricilla eyed the digital glow of the hotel clock. "They're serving dinner in twenty-five minutes."

"I'll have to come back at least two more times for fittings. Maybe three."

"That's fine." Trisha nodded at her reflection in the full-length mirror that hung on the wall. "Though, with this weekend's menu, I might not have to have the dress altered quite as much. If it's anything like lunch, I'm bound to gain a few pounds."

"You and me both." Pricilla tossed the magazine back on the table and fished her lipstick from her makeup bag. "But with food prepared by top chefs trying to impress the judges for a $250,000 cash prize, it will be worth indulging."

Riley let out a low whistle. "I could use the $250,000, though I'd never make it past boiling water in a food competition."

"And what would you do with all that cash, Riley?"

"I want to start my own line of wedding and bridesmaid dresses."

"With your talent, I wouldn't be surprised at all if you did just that one day." Pricilla flipped on the light by the desk. It flickered, then finally stayed on. She put on a layer of the lipstick and then dabbed some powder across her forehead, wondering why she even tried to cover up the decades of wrinkles. "Weren't your parents in the restaurant business, Riley?"

"They used to own a seafood restaurant called The Krab Kettle on the Oregon coast, but they sold the place five years ago," Riley said with a sigh. "Both my parents died not too long after that."

"I'm so sorry." Pricilla caught the young woman's grim expression and felt sorry she'd brought up the subject. Maude Lock, one of Pricilla's good friends, had recommended Riley and, in the course of their conversation, had mentioned that the woman's family had once owned a restaurant. She'd failed to mention that the couple was no longer living.

"I heard that the infamous Norton Richards is filling in for one of the contest judges," Riley said, changing the subject. "Is that true?"

"Yes, do you know him?" Pricilla asked.

"By reputation only."

Norton Richards had a legendary reputation. The former food critic was said to be liked by few, hated by many.

But Pricilla preferred to dismiss the gossip. "I'm hoping this weekend proves that the man isn't nearly as vicious as his reputed character."

Riley frowned. "You're far too kind, Pricilla."

"Did he ever review your parents' restaurant?" Trisha asked.

"Theirs, along with dozens of others across the country."

Pricilla snapped her powder compact shut. One thing was certain. From what she'd heard, any event including Richards was bound to be memorable.

Max Summers savored a creamy spoonful of crab bisque soup. Pricilla might have had to twist his arm to get him to attend the three-day competition, but if the main course was even half as good as tonight's appetizer, he'd have to change his tune. He glanced over at her, with her bright hazel eyes and soft, silver curls. His gaze shifted to her soup bowl. Strange. She hadn't touched her food, nor was she smiling.

He set down his spoon. "What's wrong?"

The orange glow of the elaborate candle centerpiece set up in the lodge's Great Room emphasized her solemn expression. "I'm beginning to wonder if your coming with me this weekend was a mistake, Max."

"A mistake?" He reached for a pat of butter and spread it in the middle of a hot bread roll. And she'd been the one complaining how little time they spent together. Things might change after the wedding, but in the meantime he was living in New Mexico doing his best to sell his house, while she continued working at her son's lodge in Colorado. "Why do you say that?"

Pricilla's hand stopped his spoon halfway to his mouth. "Cream-filled bisque and real butter isn't exactly on your diet."

His eyes widened as he breathed in the rich scent of the soup and felt his mouth water. He wasn't giving this up without a fight. "I'm not on a diet."

"Not technically, but have you already forgotten the doctor's report from your last checkup?" She shook her head. "This meal is nothing but high cholesterol, high fat, and high calories."

Max chuckled before downing another bite. "Must be why it tastes so good."

"Max. I'm serious."

"So am I." While he loved Pricilla despite her some-times unconventional ways, there were certain things he had no intention of changing. It was time to throw it back into her court. "Have you already forgotten that you were the one who wanted us all to come this weekend to relax and enjoy ourselves?"

Which was exactly what he was doing.

His daughter, Trisha, who sat across from them, held out a basket of rolls to Pricilla. Max smiled—the perfect diversion. Even Pricilla couldn't ignore perfectly baked bread. "He's right you know, Mom. All of us need to relax."

Max helped himself to a second roll and added it to his

plate. He was relaxing. How could he not? The atmosphere was ideal. The company perfect. And the food, well, you couldn't get much better than this.

It was undeniably the ideal location for this year's cooking contest extravaganza. A low murmur of voices, sprinkled with occasional bits of laughter, filled the lodge's Great Room where the judges, staff, and invited guests—all except the actual contestants—had gathered at the two long, formally dressed tables. Fading rays of sunlight shimmered behind the large windows overlooking the Rocky Mountains. Tomorrow the place would be buzzing with cameras and reporters, but tonight, with a fire crackling in the stone fireplace, the large room had an intimate feel.

A woman with black pants and a silver sequined blouse made her way up to the podium in the front of the room. She couldn't be over thirty-five, but her face barely moved as she glanced over the crowd with her frozen smile. Botox, no doubt, had trapped her expression as it did for thousands of others who refused to believe one could grow old gracefully. But he knew it was possible. Just a glance at Pricilla reminded him of that.

"Good evening, ladies and gentlemen." The Botox woman placed a hand on each side of the podium and leaned forward. "My name is Michelle Vanderbilt, and I'm here to represent *Food Style* magazine as we host a nationwide search for the next master chef."

A twenty-something-year-old, with mousy brown hair and a timid expression to match, snapped photos from the other side of the dining table.

"On behalf of our illustrious magazine, I want to welcome all of you to the stunning Silvermist Lodge, set in the middle of the beautiful Rocky Mountains," Miss Vanderbilt continued. "I hope you all are enjoying your dinner so far. Tonight's menu was planned and created by our six finalists as an informal kickoff before the official opening in the morning. And if tonight is any indication of what's ahead, we can all be assured that none of us will go home hungry."

Max wiped the sides of his mouth with the cloth napkin from his lap, then joined the rest of the audience in their enthusiastic applause. He'd been right. This weekend was bound to be filled with an incredible menu and nothing—not even his lovely fiancée—could stop him from enjoying it to the fullest.

"As you all know, tomorrow begins *Food Style* magazine's celebrated Rocky Mountain Chef Competition. And as one of the premiere cooking contests in the country, this year's prize is not only $250,000, but a one-year scholarship to the prestigious Parisian culinary school, Bon Appétit."

The guests applauded at the announcement.

"We have a few things to discuss before the official opening in the morning. All six of the contestants have checked in, and let me remind you that interaction between contestants and judges is strictly forbidden. Before the main course is served, I'd like to make a few brief introductions and then leave you to enjoy the rest of your meal. I'll begin by introducing our honorary emcee for the event, Pricilla Crumb. Mrs. Crumb taught home economics for thirty-two years at the esteemed Willow Hill Private Academy for Girls in Seattle and currently works as the chef at the famous Hunting Lodge and Resort in Rendezvous, Colorado."

Max nudged Pricilla with his elbow, and she held up her hand and waved as the guests clapped.

"Continuing with our judges, I'd like to welcome Manny Parker from Denver who owns Manny's Grill; Violet Peterson, owner of Le Petit Gourmand, which is also located in Denver; Lyle Simpson, *Food Style* magazine's own food critic; and celebrity chef J. J. Rhymes."

Max joined with the applause while popping a piece of bread into his mouth.

"I'd also like to extend a personal welcome to Norton Richards, renowned food critic, who has graciously agreed to take over for our fifth judge, who was unable to attend due to a last-minute family crisis."

Silence filled the room. A few scattered claps followed.

Miss Vanderbilt cleared her throat. "Lastly, I'd like to remind the judges of the informational meeting we'll be having at eight thirty tonight."

Max leaned in toward Pricilla. "What's the deal with Norton Richards?"

"Where do I begin?" she whispered. "He used to be a food critic who is said to have ruined a few good careers along the way with little regret on his side."

"That bad?"

"Let's just say you never wanted to be caught on the downside of one of his reviews. I'm not sure how true all the rumors are, but supposedly he could shut down a restaurant quicker than it takes to order a dish of crème brûlé."

Max let out a low whistle. "Ouch."

Miss Vanderbilt scanned the audience with her emotionless expression. "Enjoy the rest of your dinner."

The waiters brought out the main course next. Max's mouth watered at the sight of spicy prawns and a juicy steak. Even the vegetables looked to be cooked to perfection. He sampled a prawn and smiled. This was one of the things he looked forward to as Pricilla's husband. She could turn a bad apple into a delectable dish. He took another bite and thought of his still fairly slim waistline. Perhaps she was right. If he wasn't careful, he'd end up looking like his old fishing pal, Bud. Still, for now he planned to enjoy himself.

Dishes clattered at the other end of the table. A chair skidded across the floor. Max looked up.

"I don't have to listen to this. I don't have to listen to any of you." Norton Richards's voice rose above the chatter in the room. "I came as a favor to Miss Vanderbilt, who knew my presence would boost the ratings of this sorry contest." He threw his napkin onto the table. "But there's no way I'll stand for being treated this way."

Beside Max, Pricilla sucked in a lungful of air. Mr. Richards's chair crashed to the floor as he spun away from the table.

"Mr. Richards, please. . ."

Miss Vanderbilt's words were ignored as Norton Richards stomped from the room.

Pricilla pulled back the heavy curtain of her window. The glowing red clock beside her bed read five after twelve, but she was too keyed up to sleep. Norton's sudden exit from the dining room had startled everyone, bringing an abrupt end to the friendly camaraderie of the evening.

Apparently someone didn't like his presence here. She hadn't been able to see who the man had argued with at the dinner table, or hear what had set him off, but that didn't stop her from wondering what could have been said to have provoked such a dramatic outburst.

She tried to focus on the beauty of the quiet night. The last days of summer had already faded into autumn, bringing with it cooler nights at the higher elevations. Moonlight spilled against the circles of the half dozen hot-water pools that lay on the outskirts of the lodge. Swaying aspen trees and shadowy white light lent an eerie feel to the night.

A man shouted.

Pricilla strained to make out two shadows that appeared on the path near the pools. Without her bifocals she was forced to squint. She fumbled for her glasses, slid them on, and then turned back to the window. Two figures struggled in the moonlight, but she couldn't make out the details. Dark clothing. . .a flash of metal. . .glasses on the larger figure. . .

She shuddered.

The lifeless body of Reggie Pierce filled her mind, but she shoved it away. Reggie, and Charles Woodruff for that matter, were completely different situations. Stumbling across a murdered victim twice in her life was bad enough. Three times. . .no. Someone crying out in the night didn't mean a murder was taking place.

A second cry shattered the quiet of the night.

Pricilla pulled her robe tighter around her waist and rushed toward the hallway. If she took the side door that led outside, she could get there in a hurry. Her room wasn't far from the pools. Slowing halfway down the stairs, she fought to catch her breath and wondered why she hadn't taken the elevator. Two solved murders might have gained her a measure of respect at the Rendezvous sheriff's office, but it had done little to stop the effects of age. Her left hip groaned and her lungs begged for air. She wasn't prepared to take on a murderer.

Nor would she have to, because there was no murderer—just someone who needed help. She huffed down the stairs, the bunion on her left foot throbbing, and then stopped when she saw a shadowy image through the window at the end of the hall. Her heart caught in her throat. This was no lover's quarrel. She had to do something. She glanced down the empty corridor.

The red fire alarm caught her eye.

No. She couldn't. Or could she? Surely this qualified as an emergency. Without another thought, she pulled the handle. The alarm blasted, and water began to shower from the ceiling.

The sprinkler system?

Cascades of water ran down her face. There was no time to consider the consequences of what she'd just done. Instead, she scurried out the door and down the stone path. Lights from the rooms flickered on one by one, illuminating the garden as the siren continued to scream.

Pricilla froze at the edge of the top hot-water pool. She was too late. Clarissa Fields, one of the contestants, stood over Norton Richards's body, her hands covered in blood.

2

"Please tell me it's not true that you just stumbled across another dead body."

Pricilla's shoulders tensed at the sound of Max's baritone voice. He brushed up beside her, his sleeve wet against her bare arm. A drop of water fell from his nose. Obviously she had more to explain to him than simply how she'd managed to set off both the fire alarm and the sprinkler system. She hesitated with her response, knowing he wasn't going to like her answer. Norton Richards, she'd been told, was very much dead.

"You're soaked."

"And you're avoiding the issue." His hand brushed against her forearm. "Pricilla? What happened? The sprinkler system goes off, the police arrive to investigate an apparent murder, and now I find you out here in the middle of a crime scene?"

"This is unbelievable." A man in a bathrobe and slippers stood beside the yellow crime scene tape and addressed Pricilla. "I used to work installing sprinkler systems. Do you realize that you have more of a chance of getting hit by an asteroid than setting one off by pulling the fire alarm?"

How could news of her misdemeanor travel so quickly? Weren't there more serious matters to deal with? Like murder?

"It was an emergency. I thought—"

"Odds are something like ten million to one." The man shook his head.

"Pricilla has always been one to beat the odds." Max steered her away from the growing crowd. "Forget him. What happened?"

"Norton Richards was murdered. I found him lying at the edge of one of the hot-spring pools." Even in the shadows of the aspen trees surrounding them, she could feel his piercing gaze. She stared at the flashing lights of a police car stopped two dozen feet away at the edge of the parking lot. "Someone else must have heard the screams and called the police—they got here just after I did."

Max ran his fingers through his damp hair and sat down on a weathered bench just outside the partitioned-off crime scene. "Have you already forgotten the last time you stumbled across a dead body?"

She pushed away the lifeless image of Reggie Pierce. "I'd like to forget."

He folded his arms across his chest and caught her gaze. "Let me recap. You were arrested, knocked out, taken hostage—"

"Okay, okay." She held up her hand. "So things got a bit out of hand—"

"A *bit* out of hand? They're already out of hand this time in my opinion."

She sat down beside him. "Everything turned out fine before."

"Does that really matter?" Max let out a loud "humph." "Along with a murder, there is always a murderer. If this one is loose and thinks you can identify him. . ."

Pricilla felt her stomach clench. "The sheriff believes they already have the suspect in custody."

"Who?"

This was the problem. "When I arrived, Clarissa Fields,

one of the contestants, was standing over the body, her hands covered with blood. But I know she didn't do it."

"She didn't?"

"No."

He grasped her hand. "And how do you know that?"

"I knew Clarissa when I taught back in Seattle. She was one of my best students. I knew her family from church. I'm convinced that she's no more a murderer than your. . .than your own mother."

"Wait a minute." Max shook his head. "I'm not accusing anyone, but you're telling me that a man was found with someone standing over him, and she was covered in blood? What more evidence do you need?"

She shrugged, wishing she had a more concrete answer. "All I know is that Clarissa didn't do it."

Max fiddled with her diamond engagement ring. "The police will take her down to the station and question her. If she's innocent, they'll find that out on their own. They don't need your help."

"So you'd let an innocent girl get locked up for life on murder charges for a crime she didn't commit?"

"That won't happen." His mouth tightened. "Trust the system this time, Pricilla. I don't want you getting involved."

She frowned. "It's not as if I did any of this on purpose. I was standing at the window of my room and heard someone shouting, so I came outside to see if I could help."

An officer approached them in his regulation forest green button-down uniform shirt, with a shoulder patch that said Deputy across the top. "Mrs. Crumb?"

Pricilla's stomach began to churn, and she was quite

certain this problem wouldn't be remedied with a handful of antacid tablets. There had to be a law about pulling the fire alarm, or setting off the sprinkler system for that matter. No doubt the man was kind enough to spare her the embarrassment of arresting her in front of her friends.

"I take full responsibility for my actions, Deputy. Pulling the alarm was a foolish and impulsive act. If you want to arrest me. . ." She held out her hands in defeat.

"I haven't had a chance to talk to the manager, but considering the circumstances, I'd imagine that he'd prefer a few wet carpets to a murderer loose on the premises."

"But I'm certain there still is a murderer loose. Clarissa didn't kill Norton Richards."

"Pricilla."

She ignored Max's pointed plea. "She couldn't have."

"So you are acquainted with Clarissa Fields?" The eager look on the deputy's face implied he was ready to wrap up another case.

She frowned. It was time this cowboy slowed down.

"I've known her for years, in fact. I'm an old friend of her family."

"Then the sheriff will want to speak to you briefly, if you don't mind waiting in the lobby for a few minutes."

"Of course not."

He nodded his head and started to walk away.

"Wait a minute." Pricilla hurried toward him, ignoring the throbbing in her hip from hustling down the stairwell. "Are you arresting Clarissa?"

"She's being taken to the sheriff's office for questioning."

"But I know she didn't do it."

The deputy stopped, hands planted firmly against his hips. "Do you have evidence that implicates another person?"

She pressed her lips together. "No."

"Evidence speaks louder than feelings, Mrs. Crumb."

"What about a murder weapon?"

"We are still investigating this murder."

"All I know is that Clarissa isn't capable of murder."

"Ma'am, when you've worked for the department as long as I have, you discover that everyone has a secret. And those secrets lead to all kinds of violence." He tipped his wide-brimmed hat. "The sheriff will meet you in the lobby in five minutes."

Pricilla glanced across the yellow tape line where Clarissa stood with the sheriff. One of the white outdoor lights from the garden revealed long, reddish-brown hair pulled back from her face in a neat ponytail. Her white T-shirt was smudged with blood on the front. The girl looked up at Pricilla. Her complexion had paled to a chalky white. Fear shone in her eyes.

"Mrs. Crumb?" She took a step forward, but the officer stopped her.

Pricilla approached the tape. "May I talk to her?"

"Pricilla." Max grasped her elbow.

"No one can speak to her now," the officer said. "We're taking her down to the station for questioning."

"I didn't stab Mr. Richards, Mrs. Crumb. Please. Promise you'll help me."

"You know I'll do whatever I can."

As the officer led Clarissa to the car, Pricilla melted onto the bench beside Max. "I know I sound crazy, but she didn't do it."

"And you shouldn't get involved." Max stiffened beside her. "And you shouldn't have promised that you'd help her."

But she had, because the authorities were making a mistake. They were missing some clue from the scenario that would be revealed in the light of day. The ambulance pulled out of its parking space, followed by the squad car containing Clarissa. One thing wouldn't change. The medical examiner had arrived, taking with him from the scene Norton Richards in a body bag. There was no denying the fact that someone had taken his life, nor the fact that Clarissa's hands had been covered with the man's blood. Still. . .

Pricilla scanned the growing crowd of spectators that gathered just outside the yellow tape. Clarissa was no murderer. She knew it. Her instincts for people rarely proved her wrong, and she was certain tonight wouldn't be an exception.

Max had insisted on joining Pricilla and the sheriff for the interview. The manager of the hotel had opened up his office to them so they could talk in private and had even brought in a pot of tea. While Max was normally a coffee drinker, the mug of tea gave him something to do besides worry about Pricilla.

When this was over, he planned to sit down with Pricilla and insist she stay out of the case. He had no intention of being an overbearing husband, but when murder was involved, he felt he had the right to put his foot down. Just because things had turned out okay in the past didn't mean they would this time.

Pricilla sat beside him with a cup of steaming tea in her hands, looking more relaxed than he'd expected. Her hair was a bit damp, but her eyes were alert. Truthfully, it was this trait of always wanting to help others that had made him fall in love with her. If only that same attribute didn't always manage to land her in so much hot water.

The sheriff, looking agitated, cleared his throat and pressed the palms of his hands against his tan trousers. "I'm sorry to have to question you so late, but I find it best to talk to witnesses while the scene is fresh in their minds."

"I understand." Pricilla set her tea down on the small end table beside her and crossed her legs.

"How well did you know Clarissa?"

"I've known her since she was about five. Her parents moved to Seattle, where I lived at the time. From Baltimore, I believe."

"What can you tell me about her family?"

Pricilla paused to consider the question. "Let's see. Her parents divorced before they moved to Seattle, so I knew her mom and stepfather. She was an only child, and both sets of grandparents have passed away since I first met them. I also remember that she used to spend summers with her aunt, her mother's sister, back East when she was younger."

Max listened to each question, all thoroughly routine and professional. He'd spent half his life in the military learning how to negotiate, talk peace, and delegate responsibilities, but seeing Pricilla involved once again in a murder investigation left him with knots in his stomach.

If anything happened to her. . .

"Do you have any idea if she might have known Mr. Richards?" The sheriff's tea lay untouched beside him.

"I wouldn't know."

"When's the last time you saw her?"

Pricilla glanced at Max. Was that a sign of guilt in her expression?

She looked away. "About four years ago, right before she left Seattle to work in California."

Aha. How well could she know a person she hadn't seen for that long?

The sheriff cleared his throat and squirmed in his chair. "That's quite awhile, you know. People can change."

"Not Clarissa. She was always a hard worker and very conscientious." Pricilla leaned forward. "Listen. I know you see me as just another civilian witness. An old lady who doesn't know what she's talking about, but I have experience—"

"Pricilla." Max felt his jaw tense. Surely she wasn't planning to bring up Reggie Pierce.

"Please, Max." She rested her hand on his arm. "I want to see the truth, as much as I want to see Clarissa released. You see, I've worked on a couple cases as an unofficial consultant for the sheriff's office back in Rendezvous."

Max shook his head. So much for insisting she not get involved.

The sheriff's brow rose. "You were an unofficial consultant?"

"Just think about it. You want the truth, and I'm in the perfect position to help you find it. I'm one of the only people involved in the contest who can freely speak to the judges, the staff, and the contestants."

He rubbed his chin. "I don't know."

"I'd let you know right away if I found out anything pertaining to the case."

"Please know that I do understand your concern, Mrs. Crumb. And while I appreciate your offer, and I'm sure that you have Clarissa's best interests in mind, I have to go back to the simple fact that a civilian working on a case isn't acceptable."

The sheriff cleared his throat and then stood to shake their hands.

Max smiled. Good. The interview was over, and the sheriff had made his position clear.

Max felt Pricilla stiffen beside him as the man left the room. "He's right, you know."

Loud voices from the lobby interrupted any response Pricilla might have tried to throw back at him. Michelle Vanderbilt, still dressed in her sequined top and black pants, stood at the front counter talking to the manager. Water from the woman's hair dripped on the floor while black makeup smeared beneath her eyes like a raccoon, making Max suddenly grateful he wasn't the one having to deal with the overbearing woman.

When Michelle saw the sheriff emerge from the office, she skittered across the wood floor in her high heels, dragging her assistant with her. "I need to know exactly what's going on. I'm in charge of coordinating this nationally-televised competition, and if the sprinkler system going off wasn't bad enough, news of a murder connected to the competition will leak out and ruin our ratings."

"Or draw viewers to you like flies to manure on a hot summer day," Max commented under his breath.

Pricilla nudged him with her elbow. "Max."

"Have you seen the way she treats her assistant?" he murmured.

"Sarah?"

"I saw her yelling at the poor girl earlier. She doesn't seem to hesitate saying what's on her mind. No matter what it is."

"The woman's under a lot of pressure to make sure everything flows smoothly the next three days. You can hardly blame her for being on top of things."

The sheriff stopped in front of the woman. "I'm sorry, Miss. . ."

"Miss Vanderbilt. Michelle Vanderbilt." She reached out her hand to shake the lawman's. "I represent *Food Style* magazine, one of the country's leading publications, as we host a nationwide search for the next master chef in the Rocky Mountain Chef Competition. Surely you've heard of it?"

Max stifled a laugh. The woman sounded like an infomercial.

"I have just voiced my concerns to the manager," she continued, barely taking a breath. "We chose this lodge, and the town of Silvermist, in an effort to bring a small-town, cozy atmosphere to our competition, but since my arrival, I've been greeted with nothing but hassles. Not only was I put into a regular room instead of the suite I requested because, for some mysterious reason, there wasn't an available upgrade, but room service is slow, and now the sprinkler system has gone off in part of the building because, I'm told, of faulty wiring. Just look at my hair. There's not even a decent hairstylist within fifty miles who can fix this."

"A man was murdered, Miss Vanderbilt—"

"Which is exactly why I'm speaking to you. I will not allow your lack of diligence and an inability to prevent murder, of all things, to mar the magazine's reputation, or my reputation for that matter."

Max leaned toward Pricilla. "This is probably the first murder this town's seen in years, and she's spouting off like we're in a war zone."

"I assure you, ma'am, that we will do all we can to ensure your show continues without interruption." The sheriff turned to the lodge manager. "But with that said, I'm afraid I'm going to have to ask everyone to stay on the hotel premises or speak to me before they leave. And I'll need a list of all the guests and staff. Tomorrow we'll start doing interviews."

"Interviews?" Michelle gripped the edge of her beaded handbag. "Why?"

Max couldn't help but smile as he spoke loud enough for the woman to hear him. "Because we've all just become suspects in a murder investigation."

Pricilla entered the dining room at halfpast seven the next morning, wishing she'd remained in bed under the warmth of the thick comforter. The last thing she felt like doing was pasting on a smile for a television audience. Already, the large room was filled with reporters, bright lights, and cameras.

Cameras that put ten pounds on a person.

She glanced at the buffet table and sucked in her stomach, hoping the tan color of her new pantsuit didn't add any inches. Bowls of fresh fruit lay beside piles of sausage, biscuits and gravy, and scrambled eggs. No. She'd definitely skip breakfast this morning. Besides the calories, the smell of food that filled the room made her stomach churn. Stumbling over murder victims late at night tended to do that.

Stifling a yawn, she poured herself a cup of black coffee from a carafe, hoping the caffeine would kick in quickly. She'd slept little last night, although looking around, it seemed she wasn't the only one who'd been unable to sleep after all the commotion. The room was already half full, but no one seemed to be moving at full speed.

Michelle Vanderbilt stood in the far corner of the room wearing a lime green skirt and matching jacket. Hands waving, she argued with the sheriff about something. She must have been right about the lack of hairdressers in the area because her blond, highlighted hair didn't look near as chic as it had yesterday.

Of course after last night's episode with the renegade sprinkler system, even Pricilla wished she could sneak away for one of her weekly visits to Iris's Beauty Salon for a touch-up. Thankfully, Trisha had managed to tame her silver curls so they looked acceptable for her upcoming stint in front of the camera. Or so she hoped.

"Good morning." Max stepped up beside her with a plate piled high with every no-no from the doctor's list. He jutted his chin toward the sparring couple. "I see the tyrant's at it again."

Obviously, any lack of sleep had done little to curb his appetite or sense of humor, but for once she wasn't in the mood to nag at him over either. There were too many other things to worry about. "Sleep well?"

He led the way to an empty table toward the back of the room. "Off and on. I'm thankful the sprinklers didn't go off in the rooms, because I'm planning a nap between interviews with the sheriff. Though I suppose someone's in a lot of trouble for not doing their job properly. Apparently, the wiring's a mess."

Pricilla slid into the seat beside him, tired of the constant reminders of the incident even if it wasn't completely her fault. Even the deputy's assurances that no charges would be pressed over her reckless act weren't enough to erase the guilt she felt over her impulsiveness. After last spring's experience with a stolen ATV, she thought she'd learned the dangers of being impulsive.

Apparently I still have a long way to go, Lord.

Her stomach growled, and she snagged a blueberry muffin from Max's plate. Another impulsive act, perhaps, but fainting in front of the camera from not eating would surely be worse than looking a few pounds heavier.

The commotion up front increased.

Max quirked his left brow. "That woman doesn't give up, does she?"

"I don't know." Pricilla didn't try to curb the sarcasm in her voice. "It could have something to do with the fact that someone told her we're all murder suspects."

"And I thought she was upset because someone turned on the hall sprinklers last night and ruined her hair."

"Max."

"Sorry, but you have to admit that the woman's difficult."

"She is a bit overbearing."

"And rude and heartless."

Tossing aside all resolutions to not overindulge over the course of the weekend, Pricilla dabbed a fat pat of real butter in the center of the muffin. A little comfort food couldn't hurt. "Personally, I'd like to cancel the entire show. I'm about ready to open the dessert competition, and I have no idea how to proceed with one man dead and Clarissa not only disqualified as a contestant but now in jail for murder."

She was worried about Clarissa. The girl lying in some dingy jail cell overnight was a frightening image she couldn't shake.

"You'll do great." He squeezed her hand. "Just forget everything that happened last night. The sheriff's department is perfectly able to handle the case and find out the truth. All you have to do is go up there and look gorgeous."

"Funny."

She bit into her muffin and started praying that God would give her a nonimpulsive plan to prove Clarissa's innocence.

"Ladies and gentlemen, I'd like to welcome you to the Fifteenth Annual Rocky Mountain Chef Competition."

Pricilla smiled at the audience while trying to ignore the red RECORD light that meant every word she spoke—and every pound and wrinkle on her body—would soon be transmitted and played in thousands of homes across the country. "I'm Pricilla Crumb, and our first competition of the day will be the dessert category."

The applause from the large crowd of spectators who had booked spaces in the audience for the weekend rang across the room. Behind her, the five contestants stood ready at their stations, outfitted in the required chef coats, black pants, aprons, and signature chef hats.

"For those of you who are watching for the first time, I'll explain the rules as we go along. For this morning's competition, all the components of the dessert must be made on-site. Each individual has four hours to make five unique desserts. During this time, judges will be assessing the contestants for their efficiency in using ingredients as well as the cleanliness of their working conditions. With monetary prizes totaling $250,000, the competition goes beyond a simple sampling of the delicacies and includes presentation, artistry, and kitchen management."

She caught Max's gaze, thankful he was in the audience. It didn't matter what had happened last night. She could do this. Adjusting her bifocals, she continued to read the prompter. The audience chuckled on cue at her first joke. So far so good. All she had to do was get through the next forty-five seconds, smile graciously after her closing remarks, and make a graceful exit.

"Lastly, I want to recognize our wonderful sponsor, *Food Style* magazine, and Michelle Vanderbilt, who have worked to make this competition the renowned event it has become." Pricilla smiled graciously on cue. "Let the competition begin."

The red light on the camera went off. She let out a sigh of relief. Turning around, she stepped away from the podium, careful not to stumble on one of the dozens of cords lying across the floor. Graceful and self-assured, she pushed her shoulders back. Max was right. All she needed to do was focus on her responsibilities for the next three days.

The sheriff signaled to someone from the wings. Pricilla moved off the stage as Miss Vanderbilt whispered something to the lawman, and he took his place in front of the audience.

The sheriff cleared his throat and tapped on the microphone. "Before the competition officially starts this morning, I feel it necessary to make several reminders. We are continuing with our interviews this morning."

Miss Vanderbilt's red lips pressed into a frown as the sheriff continued speaking. She obviously wasn't happy with the fact that the sheriff had now taken over her show, even if it was temporary. She jerked around and rushed off the stage area.

"Miss Vanderbilt—" Pricilla tried to warn her, but it was too late.

Miss Vanderbilt's heel caught on one of the cords. A camera flashed. Pricilla blinked. The younger woman's lean frame spilled across the floor.

So much for graceful exits.

Pricilla rested the ice pack against Michelle's wrist. The hotel kitchen wasn't the best place to treat an injury, but it was out of the way of the competition and had plenty of ice.

"Ouch!"

"Sorry." Pricilla moved back and let Michelle hold the pack in place. "It's going to be sore for a while."

Michelle wiped her hand across her cheek. Was the woman actually crying?

"Everything's going to be okay, you know."

"No, it's not." Michelle sniffled and then ran her fingers through her hair. "I'm going to lose my job over this entire fiasco. As if there wasn't already enough stress just trying to enforce the rules on the contestants, now I'm having to deal with a murder."

"Which rules?"

"I caught Freddie Longfellow talking with Lyle Simpson, one of the judges, who then quickly assured me that their conversation hadn't gone any further than discussing an exchange of their suitcases that had been swapped by the bellboy."

"I suppose that's understandable."

"Maybe, but not only is the reputation of the magazine and the competition on the line, but mine as well." She brushed an invisible speck from her skirt. "Though it's not as if I plan to work for *Food Style* magazine forever."

"Really?"

"The magazine, this entire competition. . ." She waved her injured hand toward the Great Room and then winced. "They're simply rungs on the ladder to get me where I want to be."

"Which is?"

"A news anchor of a major network." Michelle cocked her head, looking surprised, as if Pricilla should somehow know. "You really think I've worked all these years for. . . for this?"

"Honestly, I wouldn't know. Seems as if you've already achieved a lot in your life to me."

When Michelle didn't respond, Pricilla glanced across the busy kitchen area where staff members were doing prep work for the lunch crowd. Where was Michelle's assistant? Maybe Sarah would be able to calm her boss's fears. While Pricilla didn't think the wrist was broken, she'd asked the assistant to arrange for transportation to the doctor.

With no sign of Sarah, she poured a glass of water from the tap and handed Michelle two aspirin from her purse.

The woman downed the medicine and then smacked the glass against the counter. "And you know that all this is Norton Richards's fault, that two-faced weasel."

Now here was an interesting position. Placing all the blame on the murder victim.

Pricilla raised her eyebrows. "How could it be his fault? He's the one lying dead in the morgue."

Michelle dipped her chin. "You obviously didn't know Norton. I knew he'd go to his grave dragging others with him, and it looks like I was right."

Pricilla couldn't help but jump through the door Michelle had just left wide open. What could a few well-posed, investigative questions hurt? She'd proceed cautiously.

"So, were you and Mr. Richards friends?"

"Friends?" Michelle leaned her head back against the wall. "Norton didn't have friends. He had enemies."

"But you knew him?"

Her laugh came out more like a "humph." "Everyone who was anyone in the food industry knew the man. Newspapers and magazines wanted his columns; chefs wanted his respect and five-star reviews. Even nightly news ratings went up with a story about him, so reporters were always digging up something new. He took a few people to the top with him, but most he simply dragged through the gutter then dumped in the sewer when he was finished. The very same thing he's doing with my career even now."

Ouch. So the woman didn't like him. Considering the man's reputation to tick off everyone he came in contact with, that in itself wasn't a motive for murder. But if she had a personal vendetta against him, that might put things in a bit of a different light.

"What motive could he possibly have for wanting to ruin your career?"

"Haven't you been listening?" She blew out an exasperated sigh. "The man didn't need motives, permission, or even a valid reason for that matter. He thrived on making other people's lives miserable."

So much for wanting to believe the man's sordid reputation was simply a rumor, but sometimes the truth did hurt. How many of those taken down by a harsh review from Norton Richards deserved exactly what they got? Surely a man couldn't build a career as one of the country's foremost food critics without telling the truth, as ruthless as his approach might be. One didn't have to like the man to respect his talent. If that was indeed what it was called.

Pricilla searched for her next question. "Where did you first meet him?"

Michelle's laugh competed with the banging of pots and pans and butter sizzling on the stove. With the mouth-watering smells filling the room, missing breakfast might have been a mistake.

"I met Norton at a funeral, believe it or not. One of the editors of the magazine died last year, and he actually showed up to pay his regards."

"Who do you think killed him?"

She shot Pricilla a piercing gaze. "You think I killed him, don't you?"

"No. No, of course not. I was just wondering. There seems to be plenty of people with motives when it comes to Norton. . . ."

Pricilla looked up and immediately closed her mouth. The sheriff stood in front of her, arms folded across his chest. "Mrs. Crumb, could I have a word with you? In private?"

"Of course. I was just. . ." Her heart thudded in her chest. Just what? Interrogating a suspect after she'd specifically been told to stay away from the case? That answer would go over well. "I was helping Miss Vanderbilt. She fell and sprained her wrist."

"I am sorry, Miss Vanderbilt. I understand that the hotel is arranging transport to take you to the doctor?"

"Yes, thank you."

"Good. Then Mrs. Crumb. If you don't mind coming with me."

She minded, all right, but what choice did she have? It wasn't as if she'd done anything wrong, or even illegal. This was a free country, and no one could stop her from asking a few simple, albeit personal, questions that might or might not have any relevance to the case.

She followed the officer down the hall toward the lobby in silence, working to keep up with his long stride. Already the staff was using large vacuums to dry the carpet, making any conversation impossible to hear over the noise. It was just as well. She wasn't sure she wanted to hear what the man had to say or find out how she'd managed to get pushed to the top of his interrogation list.

Today's interview room had been set up in one of the small conference rooms. It was as cold and sterile as a jail cell.

She decided to start the conversation. "When can I see Clarissa?"

"Maybe tomorrow. I'll let you know. She's just been charged with the murder."

Pricilla plunged forward, hoping she wasn't saying something she would later regret. "Clarissa's not guilty."

"Now about Michelle," the sheriff began, ignoring her outburst.

"I was just making conversation with her."

"By asking her if she knew who killed Richards?" He held up his hand. "It's okay."

"What's okay?"

"I took the liberty of calling Detective Raymond Carter last night. I've known the man for a decade, and. . .well. . .while I'm still not too keen about the idea of working with a civilian, there are certain circumstances that have made me reconsider your offer. And as you've just shown me, you're in the perfect position to talk to people without the intimidation of a badge."

"Oh." Pricilla sat back in her chair. Twelve hours ago her involvement wasn't even an option, and now she was being given free rein to investigate? Something wasn't right. "Why the change of heart? You were fairly adamant yesterday that I should stay out of your way. No exceptions allowed."

"Well, for starters. . ." He coughed and tapped his fingers against the gray, speckled conference table. "My reelection is coming up, and I won't have my opponent speaking out against me and the crime rate. You understand, don't you?"

"Of course."

She did understand. For the most part, anyway. But there was something he wasn't telling her. A recently surfaced clue? A piece of evidence pointing to someone else? Or maybe he was telling the truth, and he just wanted her to help him solve the case so he didn't lose his reelection.

The tapping on the table continued. "Carter told me how successful you'd been in working with his department."

Pricilla bit her lip. A compliment from Detective Carter wasn't something to dismiss lightly, but Max was not going to like this.

"What exactly are you saying, Sheriff?"

"To put it bluntly, Mrs. Crumb, I need an inside source. And you're my only candidate."

bsolutely not, Pricilla." Max held up his hand in
protest as if this action would intensify the impact
of his words.

Pricilla frowned from behind the round table where
they sat near the front of the room, watching the morning
competition progress. After two hours, the plated
dessert contest was at the halfway mark. The fragrances
of chocolate, cinnamon, and vanilla filled the air, but
at the moment, her attention was far from the dessert-
laden countertops and thick sauces that bubbled on the
stovetops.

"Max—"

"Please." He leaned forward and lowered his voice.
"No matter what the sheriff told you, tracking down a
killer—again—is out of the question."

Pricilla tried to gather her poise as she absorbed
Max's too-loud protests. With the attention focused on
the competition, no one in the audience seemed to notice
his outburst, but that didn't stop Pricilla from cringing.
While it was true that the last thing she had expected this
morning was Sheriff Lewis's invitation to help solve the
case—albeit in an unofficial capacity—she also hadn't
expected Max's objections to be quite this strong.

Not that she didn't appreciate his concern over her
becoming involved in another murder. It was true that her
past experiences in solving crimes had been quite eventful,
but in the end the price she'd paid had been worth it.
Justice had been served and the real murderers locked up.

And like Reggie Pierce's case, she couldn't get around the fact that with Clarissa involved, this case had an added personal element.

"Max, I really do understand your trepidation." The last thing she felt like was arguing, but on the other hand there was a young woman's future at stake. "But you can't honestly expect me to walk away from Clarissa's plight without doing anything."

"Of course not, but—"

"And the sheriff has personally asked for my input in the case."

He folded his arms across his chest. "In an unofficial capacity only."

"Completely unofficial," she conceded. "But even you have to admit that I'm in the perfect position to talk to the judges, the contestants, and the staff who might be involved."

"Which is exactly why I don't want you involved." He leaned forward. "I have. . .concerns."

"Concerns?" Her frown deepened.

Frankly, she had concerns as well. If Clarissa was innocent, there was a murderer on the loose, and she didn't want an encounter with someone who obviously didn't think twice about ending another person's life. But concerns aside, she had promised Clarissa that she would do whatever she could. And she meant to keep her word.

Pricilla searched for a diplomatic approach to make her point. "Clarissa's life is at stake, Max, and besides, I promise not to get myself into any trouble."

"That's impossible." Max shook his head and frowned. "Pricilla, we've barely been here twenty-four hours, and you've already set off the sprinkler system and landed yourself smack-dab in the middle of a murder investigation. If that's not trouble, then I don't know what is. And if I remember correctly, I heard that very same promise before with Reggie's and Charles Woodruff's investigations—"

"Those situations were different," she insisted.

"How?"

She paused, trying to come up with a legitimate response. "I wasn't asked to help by law enforcement for one thing."

The truth was, she would prefer not to relive the dreadful moments leading up to the discovery of those murders. Instead, she turned her attention to the large viewing screen that had zoomed in on one of the contestants, Maggie Underwood, who was pulling a 9-inch spring pan filled with a chocolate cake from the oven. Pricilla's heart skipped a beat as the young woman fumbled with the hot pan, finally placing the dessert on the counter.

Pricilla let out a sigh of relief. Obviously she wasn't the only one affected by last night's tragedy. Still, despite the somewhat subdued atmosphere, the audience did seem to be enjoying watching the chefs as they whipped, stirred, and concentrated on the tiniest of details to catch the judges' attention.

She couldn't say the same for her and Max. She'd planned to enjoy her weekend, not endure a lengthy inquisition.

"And there is something else that bothers me," Max continued.

Pricilla turned back to him, praying the morning wouldn't end in a fight. "What is that?"

"If you ask me, it seems quite clear that this is an open-and-shut case. How can you argue with the evidence, especially when you were the one first on the scene? Face it, Pricilla. Clarissa was found standing over Norton's body after midnight and covered in blood. What other reason would she have had to be outside at that time on the night before the biggest competition of her life begins?"

Even Pricilla had to admit he had a point, but that didn't lessen the resolve she felt that Clarissa must have had a legitimate reason to have been there. She just wasn't sure what it was. "There has to be a perfectly logical explanation. If I had been the one to stumble across Norton's body in the dark, I would have tried to verify whether he was alive or not and in the process might have gotten his blood all over me."

"You're grasping for straws. Face it, Pricilla." Max shook his head. "You haven't seen Clarissa and her family for several years. Who's to say that Clarissa hasn't changed? People do change, and not always for the better."

She frowned. "You're sounding quite pessimistic."

"No, realistic. And you know it's only because I care." Max took her hand. He might be strongly opinionated, but all it took was one touch to remind her of why she said yes to his proposal of marriage. He made her feel young again—no matter what her bunion was telling her at the moment. "I'm just concerned about your safety, nothing more."

She matched his smile. There was already enough tension in the room—they didn't need to add a mis-understanding between themselves to the mix. "I know."

The screen switched to a close-up of a layered cheesecake, and despite the seriousness of their conver-sation, Max's expression confirmed he was already anticipating the sample-sized portions that would be handed out to the audience.

But she wasn't done yet. "All I plan to do is ask a few discreet questions."

"Discreet questions?" Max chuckled. "The problem is I remember your previous attempts at interviewing suspects. A barroom brawl and subsequent arrest is far from discreet."

"Would it help if I said I've learned my lesson?"

"No."

"Max. . ."

He let out a deep sigh. "Then humor me, Pricilla. Anything outside the lines of questioning gets run by the sheriff first. He's the one responsible for following up on any and all leads."

"I promise."

He didn't look convinced. "I can't help it. I didn't like it the first time you went head-to-head with a murderer, and I don't like it any better today. If you would only—"

A muffled cry interrupted Max. Pricilla's gaze snapped back toward the screen. Someone in the audience gasped. The smell of burnt sugar filled the room.

The cameras zoomed in on Maggie, who was in the process of grabbing a pan from the stove and dumping its contents into the sink. The audience silenced as the scorched liquid slid from the pot and down the drain.

So much for the raspberry sauce.

Pricilla couldn't help but feel sorry for the girl. A move like that most likely ruined any chances of winning. Pricilla adjusted her bifocals. Maggie turned the tap on and thrust her hand beneath the water. Even without the aid of the cameras, it was obvious the young woman had burned her hand. Pricilla rushed toward her to help, wondering what else could go wrong this weekend.

———

"It was going to be a chocolate mousse cake," Maggie said between sobs.

Pricilla had led her away from the intense stares of the audience and into the hotel kitchen where she'd doctored Michelle just a couple of short hours ago. One murder and two contestants out in less than twenty-four hours. She didn't like the odds of this game so far.

Maggie wiped her nose with her uninjured hand and sucked in a breath. "I'd even made these cute little chocolate sticks. . .and spun sugar spirals. . .but the raspberry sauce. . ." With her hand still beneath the cool running water, the crying started again.

Pricilla couldn't help but sympathize. In a normal competition, with the stakes as high as they were, the stress levels were tremendous for the contestants. Add a murderer on the loose, and who wouldn't be edgy?

"I don't even know how it happened," Maggie sniffed.

"How what happened?" Pricilla pulled the girl's hand away from the tap water to examine the burn. No blisters were present, and the redness was already almost gone.

"I've made this recipe dozens of times at my uncle's restaurant," Maggie continued. "Everybody loves it. . .and I've never burned it."

"You're just nervous, sweetie. The competition's stressful, and then there's the murder on top of all of that. . . ."

Fresh tears brewed in Maggie's eyes. Pricilla obviously shouldn't have brought up the murder. She glanced at her watch. "Listen, there's still almost an hour and a half left in the competition."

Whether that was enough time, Pricilla wasn't sure, but it was at least worth a try. She patted the small wound with a cloth and handed Maggie a couple of pain relievers. "You can still try."

"I don't know, Mrs. Crumb." Maggie fiddled with the edge of her chef's hat.

"If you ask me, you've come too far to simply give up now."

Maggie sniffled again and nodded her head. "I suppose you're right." She jumped off the barstool and headed back to her station.

The sheriff entered the room as Pricilla was leaving. "It seems like every time I run into you, Mrs. Crumb, you're playing the role of medic."

"Something I'm certainly not, though perhaps we need to open a nurse's station beside your investigation room with all that's happened in the past twenty-four hours."

As they entered the Great Room, Pricilla watched Maggie step into her kitchen, take a deep breath, and start back to work. The audience cheered her return. Pricilla hoped it would be enough to keep her in the competition.

The sheriff folded his arms across his chest and sighed. "I'm on my way to the lobby to meet with the manager. Do you have a few minutes to walk with me?"

"Of course." Pricilla couldn't help but notice the difference between Sheriff Lewis and the small town of Rendezvous' Deputy Carter, who had been anything but happy at her involvement in the two murder cases back home. Obviously the deputy's tune had changed.

So much, in fact, that he'd even recommended her to the sheriff, something that still surprised her.

"I can't help but think that there is something very odd about this whole scenario," the sheriff began as they started down the hallway.

"You mean with Maggie?" Pricilla asked, not certain where the man was headed.

"How could a professional cook simply forget about her sauce?"

She pressed her lips together. Maybe Maggie had been hinting at something more than just burned sauce. "Maggie did seem genuinely perplexed as to how her sauce could have burned. What if this didn't occur because she was nervous and simply forgot? She's made the dessert dozens of times and knows what she's doing."

He rubbed his chin with his fingers, obviously trying to connect the dots, something Pricilla had yet to do. "So you're saying she implied someone had been tampering with her equipment."

"Not in so many words. . .but now that I think about it, that was the impression I got."

"Is it possible?"

"I suppose. There are rules set up to keep people out of the kitchens, but if someone has enough motivation, they could find a way around them."

"So someone could have tampered with her equipment. That's a pretty serious accusation."

"Except that leads to the question of motive," Pricilla said. "It doesn't make any sense, at least not in connection with Norton. It only makes sense in light of the competition."

"Maybe Maggie was distracted and burned the sauce because she has a guilty conscience," the sheriff offered.

Pricilla shrugged. Truth be told, she'd burned a few things in the course of her career as a chef. "Even professionals aren't perfect."

"Maybe, but all she needed was a moment of rage, and before she knows it, a man is dead. It's worth looking into anyway." He stopped at the edge of the lobby where complimentary beverages were being offered to the guests. "Coffee?"

Pricilla shook her head and waited while the lawman helped himself to a Styrofoam cup of the strong brew with two sugars and a cream.

"What do you know about Maggie?" He took a sip of his drink and waited for her response.

"Besides her bio in the program? Not a whole lot." Pricilla tried to remember what she'd read about the young woman. "She's twenty-eight, single, and the youngest of the group next to Clarissa. She's worked as a sous-chef for the past four years in her uncle's restaurant, Sassy's."

"I've heard of it. That's a pretty classy joint."

"From what I've seen so far, she knows what she's doing and is good at it. Before today's incident, I would have placed her near the top of the contenders. A mistake like that, though, could mean that the competition is pretty much over for her."

"What else?"

Pricilla shrugged. "She seemed nervous on camera today, and while this isn't her first competition, the stress level for all the contestants is high. Not to mention that someone was murdered last night."

"So you think her reaction today is nothing more than nerves?"

Pricilla shrugged, wishing she could give him more. "I don't know."

"What about a connection to Richards?" the sheriff continued.

"None that I know of, though I'm quite certain Norton would have done a review of her uncle's restaurant at one time or another." Pricilla paused. "Still, considering all the bad reviews the man wrote, it's a miracle he lasted this long."

"So you think we're looking at revenge."

"Maybe. What I do know is that you're looking in the wrong place with Clarissa."

"Something you've mentioned at least once or twice already." The man looked away, lost it seemed, in his own evaluation of the case. "The DA wants to wrap this one up quickly."

"As do you."

"So you'll keep your eyes and ears open?" the sheriff asked.

"You know I will." Pricilla paused, wanting to turn the tables before their interview was over. "But there is one other thing I'd like to know."

"What's that?"

"Did Clarissa give you a reason for her being out last night?"

The sheriff glanced around the lobby, which was empty except for a desk clerk and a couple waiting by the front door. "You have to understand, Mrs. Crumb, that anything I tell you must be kept between us in the strictest of confidences."

"Certainly."

"Clarissa's lawyer has talked to her."

"What about her parents?"

"Her mother and stepfather are off on a cruise some-where in the Caribbean, and we've been unable to reach them as of yet."

"And as for her guilt?"

"She denies any involvement in the murder. Claims she couldn't sleep and decided to go for a walk. While she was coming up the path, she heard two people arguing and went around the pools to avoid them, believing that it had to be some lovers' quarrel. She heard someone yell, then saw someone running."

"And the blood?" Pricilla asked.

"She'd recently taken a CPR class. She claims she was trying to save his life."

"And you believe her." Pricilla phrased her question like a statement.

The sheriff's gaze darted to the right. "Yes. I do. And that's why I need your help. The DA doesn't agree with me. They've gone ahead and charged her."

The hotel manager emerged from a doorway behind the front desk. "Sheriff. . .Mrs. Crumb. . .I'm sorry to interrupt."

The sheriff's eye twitched. "It's fine. I was planning to come talk to you."

Pricilla started to leave.

"Before you leave, Mrs. Crumb, I want to thank you," the manager said.

"Thank me?"

"The electrical inspector's in a ruckus over the sprinkler situation. The man who worked on it is probably going to lose his license. Thankfully, you brought the problem to our attention."

Pricilla swallowed a twinge of guilt. "That wasn't exactly my plan."

The man tugged on his jacket. "I understand, but in

a real emergency, the situation could have ended up being far more serious."

"You're welcome. I think. Now if you will both excuse me."

The sheriff's gaze shot to the doorway and then back to her. "Of course, Mrs. Crumb. We can continue our conversation at a later time."

Pricilla returned to the Great Room and forced herself to concentrate on the rest of the dessert segment, certain there was something the lanky lawman wasn't telling her. She'd had the same feeling just a few hours earlier in the conference room after her interview with him but still wasn't sure why. Maggie managed to make a comeback with her chocolate mousse cake, but even that triumph wasn't enough to beat out Freddie Longfellow. As soon as the session was over, Pricilla made a point to snag Freddie in order to congratulate him on his win. . .and to take the opportunity to ask a few questions.

Her smile broadened as she approached him. She had a job to do, and there was no better time than the present. "Congratulations on winning the first round, Mr. Longfellow."

"It's Freddie, please, and thank you." He brushed a tuft of blond hair out of his eyes and smiled at her, apparently trying to transmit some of the charm to her that he'd used earlier. His flamboyant personality had captured the judges' attention as well as the audience's. "I've worked long and hard to win this competition."

"It's far from over."

"True, but this is my third time to compete, and this time I plan to win. I'll be in school in Paris this time next year."

"You sound pretty confident."

He straightened his linen jacket. "I have been told that my distinctive combinations of flavors can't be beat, and I'm counting on it."

Enough to knock off one of the judges? She wasn't ready to dismiss that question yet.

Pricilla decided to pull out the only card she had, not sure where it would lead her. "That doesn't by any chance have to do with your tête-à-tête with Lyle Simpson does it?"

Freddie cleared his throat. "Not that it really is any of your business, Mrs. Crumb, but before rumors start flying as to the validity of my integrity, like I assured Miss Vanderbilt, the bellboy switched my bags with Mr. Simpson's when I checked in. As the competition hadn't even started, I didn't see any harm in knocking on the man's door and retrieving my luggage. And if, for whatever reason, you don't believe my story, the bellboy will back me up."

A nice, pat story, for sure.

But he did have a point. "I'm sorry to have implied otherwise, Mr. . .Freddie."

Perhaps it was time to steer the conversation clear of accusations before she turned the man off entirely. "To be honest, this year has had a bit of a rough opening with the death of one of the judges, hasn't it? I suppose it has all of us rattled."

"I don't know. From what I've heard, the death of Norton Richards isn't too great a loss."

Pricilla grimaced at the man's blasé comment. "I've always believed that any loss of human life is great."

"True, of course, but the man did have a knack for stirring up trouble." Freddie eyed a tall blond across the room. "Or so I've been told."

Pricilla frowned. "So you didn't know Norton?"

Freddie turned his attention back to Pricilla. For the moment, anyway. "Never saw the man before last night."

Pricilla frowned. Freddie was cocky. Too cocky. And from the look on his face, their conversation was over. "It was nice to chat with you, Mrs. Crumb, but I have a phone call to make before the next competition starts."

Pricilla glanced at her watch. There was an hour and a half until the next competition began, which gave her just enough time to go upstairs to her room, brush her teeth, and perhaps slip in a ten-minute energy nap before she met Max for lunch.

Freddie headed for the blond, while Pricilla took the elevator to her floor.

When she stepped out a few moments later, someone grabbed her arm.

"Pricilla?" Trisha stood in front of her, her face pale.

Pricilla pressed her hand against her chest, with the fear that another murder had taken place. "What's happened?"

"Quick. Into the room."

Pricilla followed her down the carpeted hall, slipping in behind her.

"What in the world are you doing, sneaking about the hotel like this after a. . ."

"A murder?" Trisha paced the floor.

"Exactly. You startled me half to death."

"I'm sorry. I had no intention of scaring you, and I suppose this will seem insignificant in the light of everything that's going on, but. . ." Trisha paused. "You know my engagement ring."

"Of course. Nathan's talked about it enough for me to

have its every detail memorized. A pear-shaped diamond he handpicked in South Africa. Custom setting and gold band. . .not another one like it in the world."

"Which is precisely the problem." Trisha held up her left hand as tears welled in her eyes. "It's missing."

Pricilla grasped Trisha's bare hand in horror. Another glitch in the wedding plans wasn't going to go over well at this point, and a lost engagement ring more than fit the definition of catastrophe.

Trisha frowned. "Nathan even reminded me last week to get the ring resized. I'd planned to do it as soon as we got back home, but he was right. I should never have waited."

And he was not going to be happy with the news. The custom-made engagement ring had been designed exclusively for Trisha and couldn't be purchased online or at the mall. Not to mention the sentimental value that was worth even more than the ring itself.

Pricilla perched on the edge of the queen-sized bed and ran her fingers across the thick down comforter. The ring had to be somewhere around the hotel, but where? "When did you last see it?"

"That's the problem. I'm not sure." Trisha rubbed her fingers around the bare spot, the furrows in her brow deepening. "I noticed it was gone yesterday afternoon, but I kept praying I'd find it. I. . .I'm not sure I can tell Nathan."

Pricilla frowned. They'd have to deal with Nathan at some point, but for now Trish was going to have to narrow it down closer than sometime yesterday.

Trisha sat down across from her on the dressing table stool and clasped her hands together. "Riley commented about it yesterday during my fitting. After that, I'm not sure."

"Okay, we know you had it on then," Pricilla began.

The steps to deducing where she'd seen the ring last were no different than deducing who had murdered Norton Richards. Except at least with a murder investigation, the number of suspects could normally be narrowed down to a small handful. Finding the ring could be more like finding a needle in a haystack. But as with any good investigation, they just needed to start at the beginning. "We need to make a timeline."

"All I did yesterday was my fitting with Riley, coffee with Nathan in the restaurant, and then we went for a walk around the lake before dinner in the Great Room." Trisha rose and started pacing the tan carpet again.

A walk around the lake definitely posed a problem by widening the search perimeter. If the ring had fallen off somewhere on the trail, the haystack had just turned into a football field, and it would be nearly impossible to find. From the look on Trisha's face, the same reasoning had gone through her mind as well.

Trisha stopped at the open window that overlooked Silvermist Lake in the distance. Her face paled. "Wait a minute."

"What is it?" Pricilla joined her at the window. While she'd always enjoyed the view of the aspen trees, evergreens, and the lofty Rocky Mountains from her bedroom window at Nathan's lodge, Silvermist Lodge boasted the additional stunning scene of the lake in the forefront of the distant mountains.

Trisha pointed to the placid waters. "We walked around the jogging trail that circles the lake. It's just under three miles. We stopped for a breather, and Nathan tossed a few rocks across the surface. It was so beautiful and clear. . ."

She paused, gnawing on her bottom lip.

Pricilla didn't like where this was going. "And. . ."

"Nathan challenged me to skip a stone as many times as he could."

"Then I suppose that's the most logical place to start looking."

Trisha shook her head. "Finding it out there will be impossible."

"Maybe." Pricilla glanced at her watch. "I've got a little less than an hour and a half before I have to be back at the competition."

"We'll never find it—"

"Don't give up yet. I've got an idea."

Forty-five minutes later, Pricilla and Trisha stood at the edge of Silvermist Lake with a metal detector Pricilla had managed to secure from the lodge. Stepping over logs, brush, and wildflowers, they'd scoured the edge of the rocky lake where the engaged couple had taken a break from their walk. So far, they'd turned up five bottle caps and a penny, but there was no sign of the ring.

The frequency of the beeps increased. Pricilla reached down and dug up another coin. This time it was a nickel.

Trisha, who had said little after her initial confession, now stood along the shore of the lake with her arms folded tightly across her chest. "Where in the world did you get the idea to use a metal detector?"

Pricilla walked slowly as she swept the coil back and forth above the ground. "My husband, Marty, was a treasure hunter. Never found any great treasure besides a few coins, an old locket, and some other jewelry, but he still kept up with it throughout the years. If nothing else, it was great exercise for the two of us. We spent a good part of our holidays scouring beaches, parks, and farms across the country. He loved it."

"And you?"

"I loved being with Marty." She smiled at memories of walking along the sandy coastline with the tide tugging at her feet or tramping through the woodlands, all the time with Marty beside her. It had become something they both enjoyed doing together.

Pricilla held up her right hand to show Trisha the gold band encircling her fourth finger. "I found this Celtic ring on the East Coast one summer."

"I've noticed it before. It's beautiful."

Pricilla went back to sweeping the ground, but while the idea of using a metal detector might be novel, she was quickly beginning to regret the idea. She glanced at the water lapping against the shore beside her. No woman her age should don rubber boots and wade out into cold lake water. But that's exactly what she was about to do.

She let the detector hover above the surface of the water, careful as she took her first tentative step.

"Are you sure about this?" Trisha asked.

Pricilla nodded. "This detector is waterproof, so while we're here, we might as well search the water near the shore. It can't be that deep."

"Just be careful." Trisha continued her search along the shore, staying parallel to Pricilla. "What else did you find in your treasure hunts?"

"A rare coin worth about two hundred and fifty dollars and a handful of Civil War bullets. That was pretty much the extent of my findings. Marty found a few more things."

"I'm sure you miss Marty a lot."

"I do. But now that your father's in my life. . ." Pricilla couldn't help but smile. "God made room in my heart to find love again. Something I never thought would happen."

Pricilla inched her way along the shoreline and then moved another foot out.

"Stay near the edge, Pricilla. There's no telling when the bottom drops off, and if you fall in, you'll catch pneumonia. It's got to be freezing now that summer's over."

Pricilla's chuckle rose above the *whir* of the detector. "I seem to remember someone else falling into a lake in an attempt to impress a certain young man."

Trisha and Nathan's first, unofficial date had been to go fishing, something Trisha had never attempted before.

"I've never been an outdoor girl, but Nathan's somehow managed to add fishing and hiking to my list of leisure activities." Trisha stopped at the edge of a thick log that jutted into the water a dozen feet. "But I wasn't trying to impress Nathan. I was just determined to catch as many fish as he did. I guess it didn't work."

Pricilla caught her gaze.

Trisha laughed. "Okay. I was trying to impress him. He had me hooked that very first day. Forget about the fish."

The frequency of the beeps sped up. Pricilla had found something.

She reached into the shallow water and dug in the sand with a stick. A minute later, she pulled up another bottle cap. "At this rate, we'll have the world's largest collection."

"And no ring." The hopelessness in Trisha's expression was back.

"We'll find it." Despite her encouragement, Pricilla knew the words rang hollow.

"It's impossible, and you know it." Tears welled in Trisha's eyes. "I'm just going to have to find a way to break the news to Nathan."

Pricilla kept on, determined to find the ring despite the odds.

Trisha glanced at her watch. "You've got to get back to the lodge. I can't tell you how much I appreciate what you've done, but I'm just going to have to face the truth. The ring is gone."

"Give me five more minutes."

Max peeked into the Silvermist Café, looking for Pricilla in case she'd decided to grab something to eat. She'd told him this morning that she was planning to lie down for a few minutes before lunch, so when she didn't show up, he assumed she'd decided to take a longer nap. As long as she was back in time for the next stage of the competition, some rest would do her good.

He scanned the cozy restaurant with its antique furniture, timber ceiling beams, and picture windows overlooking the lake, turning to leave when he saw no sign of Pricilla. He wasn't worried about her. Not yet anyway. A chalkboard in the doorway announced the special of the day in colorful chalk: FILET MIGNON WITH GARLIC SHRIMP, and HOMEMADE COCONUT PIE.

Homemade coconut pie. He glanced behind him into the lobby. Still no sign of Pricilla who would, no doubt, quickly point out that he had just sampled half a dozen desserts prepared by master chefs. Still, one slice of pie wouldn't hurt. . . .

His focus snapped back to the restaurant while at the same time he tried to muster his floundering remains of willpower.

A pretty blond hostess approached him, ponytail swinging behind her, menus in hand. "Table for one?"

Max hesitated. If Pricilla ever found out he'd sneaked in for a piece of pie, she'd have him running five miles with Trisha every morning.

Unless. . .

His smile broadened. One of the contestants, Christopher Jeffries, sat alone at a corner table. Early thirties, clean-cut and soft-spoken. . .Max had been impressed with the young man's performance throughout the morning competition. He'd fared well, coming in a close second behind Freddie Longfellow with his mini fruit Pavlovas and chocolate cream puffs, desserts Max had found irresistible.

He decided to take a chance. "I'll be joining Mr. Jeffries."

Thanking the hostess, he made his way to the back of the room. The quicker the case was solved, the sooner Pricilla would be able to put it behind her, and he, in turn, could stop worrying about her. Surely a bit of investigating couldn't hurt. One never knew what a few carefully chosen questions might uncover.

He stopped at the young man's table.

"Are you up for a bit of company?" Max asked. "I'd love to ask you a few questions about the competition, if it's not a bother."

Christopher folded up the newspaper he was reading

and pointed to the extra chair. "I don't mind a bit. In fact, I should be preparing for the next round, but I needed a distraction from the contest. Are you a reporter?"

"Not at all. I'm Max Summers. My fiancée, Pricilla Crumb, who's working as the emcee, talked me into coming up for the weekend."

"Christopher Jeffries, though I suppose you already know that." He chuckled. "Are you enjoying the competition so far?"

"The food is out of this world, though for you contestants, the competition must be stressful."

"Incredibly." Christopher dropped the paper onto the table. "I knew it would be. This is the second time I've entered, though I didn't make it to this level last year."

Max nodded at the piece of coconut pie Christopher was in the process of eating. Apparently Max wasn't the only who couldn't turn down the dessert.

"Is it good?"

"Fantastic." The young man took another bite. "You'd think I'd be sick of sweets after this morning, but I walked by and couldn't resist."

The waitress stopped at the table with a glass of ice water. Ignoring the nagging comments he could hear from Pricilla in the back of his mind, Max ordered a slice of the pie for himself.

"Did you know the judge who was murdered?" he asked, jumping into the conversation headfirst once the waitress had left. "Norton Richards?"

Christopher laughed. "And I was expecting the normal questions, like, how long have you been cooking, or what made you choose a career as a chef?"

Max fidgeted in his chair. So much for being subtle.

He was losing his touch. "I. . .I suppose the murder is in the forefront of everyone's mind. It definitely is in mine."

"No doubt." Christopher took another bite of pie. "Norton was a friend of my father's actually, if you could call him that. Perhaps an acquaintance is a better word. I never spent any time with the man, but from what I heard, he didn't have any real friends."

Max settled into his chair and started to relax. "So how did your father know him?"

"He's the editor for a small newspaper back in Montana, the same town where Norton was originally from. I used to work at the paper in the summers while I was in college. We ran Norton's weekly columns. That was before he was syndicated across the country."

It was interesting how everyone seemed to have a connection to the dead man. "So did you ever have any run-ins with him?"

"No, but my father did." Christopher took a final bite and then pushed his plate aside. "The small town of Junction, where my dad runs the paper, has a well-known restaurant that draws in the summer tourists. It's run by two brothers who started the place at the end of World War II. They're famous for their buffalo steaks and baked beans.

"Readers began complaining about the harshness of Norton's reviews. He might have been from Junction, but that didn't make people any less forgiving when he began bashing Sal and Winston and their cuisine."

"So what happened?"

"My father threatened to discontinue his column if he didn't write more favorable reviews."

"And did he?"

Christopher signaled the waitress for a refill on his coffee before answering. By now, most of the customers had cleared out, leaving the room quiet except for the hum of the overhead fans. "Apparently Norton didn't allow anyone to dictate what he wrote. He never sent in another review."

"Was it detrimental to the paper?"

"Not a bit, which infuriated Norton. Or so I was told."

The connection was interesting, but certainly not enough to pin a murder on. And Christopher Jeffries seemed far from the type of person to lose his temper in a heated moment. Of course, who was Max to say whether or not there was a murderer lurking within?

The waitress slid a piece of pie across the table in front of Max and then filled Christopher's coffee mug.

Max cleared his throat and opted for another angle once she'd left. "So do you think Clarissa's guilty?"

"I have to say," Christopher said as he added two packets of sugar to his drink, "that I was surprised when the sheriff arrested her. While I'd just met her, she struck me as the sweet girl next door. Can't really see her blowing up and killing someone, but then I'm no psychologist." Christopher leaned forward. "Now Michelle is more what I'd call a viable suspect."

Max's brow rose. "Why is that?"

"She doesn't remember me, I'm sure, but I met her once. She interviewed for a position at my father's paper."

Their world just kept getting smaller and smaller. "I'm having a hard time picturing Michelle stuck in some small town in Montana."

"This was before she hit the big time with the magazine. She was building her résumé and figured a small-town paper needed an ace reporter to track down stories that would bring in more readers."

"Did she get the job?"

Christopher nodded. "But she only stayed for six weeks before quitting to work for some high-profile job in New York. Made a whole lot more dough, I'm sure."

"When was that?"

"If I remember correctly, it was right before Norton moved away from Junction."

"So Michelle and Norton knew each other?"

"Oh, yeah. They knew each other all right." Christopher drummed his fingers against the table, his expression implying they'd been far more than friends. "But she ended up leaving for New York, which I'm assuming ended any relationship they had. Michelle wasn't afraid to do whatever it took to get where she wanted to go."

Including murder? Max took another bite of the pie that suddenly didn't taste quite as good as the first. That was the answer he was going to have to find out.

Pricilla took another step forward, careful not to drift too far from the shore. While the water was less than two feet deep from where she stood, the ground quickly sloped the farther one got from the shore. The last thing she needed to do was lose her footing and fall in.

The beeping increased again. She poked at the spot with her stick, careful not to stir up too much dirt. Probably nothing more than another bottle cap.

Trisha stepped out onto the log hanging over the water. "Be careful."

"I could say the same for you, Trisha, balancing like

that. I'd prefer not to have to have to rescue you."

"I might have a tendency to clumsiness, but I have no intention of joining you in the water, especially without floaters."

Sure enough, it was another bottle cap.

It was time to give up. Jamming the stick into the sandy bottom, Pricilla paused. The stick had found something else. One last attempt wouldn't hurt, even though she was certain it was too big to be a ring. "I found something, but it's probably just a rock. One thing I learned with Marty is that most finds never live up to the anticipation of the moment."

Hands on her knees, Trisha leaned forward as far as she could on the log. "What is it?"

"I don't know."

"Pricilla?"

Her gaze jerked up as the log snapped in two, plunging Trisha into the water below.

6

Strong waves slapped against Pricilla's legs, knocking her off balance. The metal detector slid from her hands. She lunged for something to hold on to but couldn't reach the branches extending from the broken log. The next second, her feet flew out from under her.

The rocky floor of the lake rushed up to greet her, slamming into her backside, as her rubber boots filled with water. She braced herself with her arms, barely keeping her head out of the water, and managed to stand back up at the same time Trisha came to the surface, gasping for air.

Pricilla reached for Trisha's arm, afraid they would both go down again. Miraculously, they didn't.

Pricilla gulped a deep breath of relief. "Are you okay?"

Trisha pushed a strand of wet hair off her face, then spewed water from her mouth. "Besides startling me to death, nothing seems to be hurt except for my pride. But what about you? I'm so sorry. I looked down, thought I saw something flash in the sunlight, and before I knew it the log had snapped beneath me."

Relieved they were both okay, Pricilla couldn't help but snicker at Trisha's shocked expression and the fact that they must both look like a couple of wet rats. While the water only came up to midthigh, both of them were completely drenched from head to toe. Of course, being thirty years older than Trisha meant that Pricilla would be the one to pay more with bumps and bruises. At least nothing seemed broken.

"I am sorry." Trisha pressed her lips together. "You're sure nothing is strained or broken?"

Pricilla shivered and started sloshing toward the edge of the lake in her waterlogged boots that felt more like lead weights. "If anything is broken, I can't feel it yet."

"Nathan's never going to believe I did this again." With her hands placed firmly on her hips, Trisha blew out a huff. "I seem to have a knack for ruining the great outdoor adventure. Here I am marrying the owner of a hunting lodge, and I can't get near a lake without falling in."

Pricilla chuckled as she grabbed the metal detector and headed toward a large rock near the shore so she could dump the water out of her boots. "Stepping out onto a rotten log over a lake does seem to be a way to substantiate the law of gravity."

"And Murphy's Law," Trisha threw out, wringing out the bottom of her drenched shirt.

Pricilla looked down at her own disheveled outfit. Murphy's Law certainly seemed to be working for her today. How in the world was she going to make herself presentable for the next competition after tromping through the outdoors for over an hour before falling in a lake? She could already hear Max's "I told you so," but this time she could honestly tell him that their excursion had nothing to do with the murder investigation. Surely that would soften his predictable rebuttal that she had a knack for finding trouble.

The metal detector started beeping. Pricilla kicked her toe against yet another bottle cap that lay on the ground and flipped off the machine. This detector had gotten her into enough trouble today.

Still, she couldn't help but wonder what Trisha had

seen before tumbling into the water.

"What do you think it was?" she asked as she dumped the water out of her boots.

Trisha shrugged. "I don't know. Something flashed along the bottom of the lake, but I'll probably never be able to find it again."

"Where?" Pricilla shoved her boots back on, ready to rescan the area with the detector if need be.

Trisha reached to snap a stick off the fallen log and poked the stick into the water where she stood. "I don't think there's anything here." She turned back toward the shore and then stopped. "Wait a minute."

Pricilla stood. "What is it?"

"I don't know, but it's big. No wonder I saw it earlier." Trisha nudged a rock away with her shoe and reached down to pull the object out of the water.

Pricilla blinked.

Trisha held a nine-inch chef's knife in her hand. Pricilla's heart began to pulsate. The murder weapon? Norton had been stabbed. And this knife wasn't rusty. She tried to dismiss the obvious conclusions. There had to be a hundred reasons why there was a knife in the water.

But a coincidence? She didn't think so.

Pricilla took in a quick breath. "You don't think that has something to do with the murder—"

"Don't even go there." Trisha shook her head and started for the shore, still holding on to the knife. "I refuse to get involved in another murder investigation. All I plan to do is find a place to dispose of this knife so no one gets hurt."

"But it's completely possible." Pricilla eyed the chef's knife. Black handle, polished edge, laminated steel. . .she'd seen the same type of knife in several of the contestants' kitchens. "If this is the murder weapon, there's no way that Clarissa could have murdered Norton. She wouldn't have had time to dispose of the evidence."

"You're jumping to conclusions."

"Stop and think about it." Shivering, Pricilla followed Trisha onto the rocky beach, thankful no one was in sight. She really didn't want to explain to anyone why the two of them were dripping wet with mucky lake water. "If I caught her red-handed, as the authorities believe, then why was there no evidence of a weapon anywhere around?"

"I don't know. I still say you're jumping to conclusions. For all we know, this knife has been here for months." Trisha combed her fingers through her wet hair. "And not only that, we're pretty far from where the murder was committed."

Pricilla eyed the knife. Trisha was right, of course. Just because they had found a knife the day after a murder was committed didn't mean the two were connected.

On the other hand, she couldn't just dismiss the possibility that the knife was the murder weapon. That evidence alone could save Clarissa. There was only one thing to do.

Pricilla quickened her steps. "We've got to go find the sheriff."

Max stood on the wooden deck of the lodge overlooking the lake. Tables lined the area with umbrellas to shade them from the afternoon sun, and there was still no sign of Pricilla. He was starting to get worried. He'd called her room twice and even went upstairs and knocked on her door, but no one had answered.

Nathan joined him at the railing. "Did you find my mom?"

Max gnawed at the toothpick between his teeth. "No. And I can't imagine where she is."

"I can't find Trisha either." Nathan leaned against the railing beside him. "It's like they've vanished from the lodge."

Max glanced at his watch and frowned. "And Pricilla is supposed to introduce the next competition in a few minutes."

"Both our cars are still out front, so they couldn't have gone too far. Maybe they went for a walk."

"That is a possibility."

Max drummed his fingers against the rail and stared out across Silvermist Lake. Surrounded by evergreens and aspens, this area was one of the most beautiful places he'd ever visited in the Rocky Mountains, but for the moment, he couldn't relax enough to enjoy the scenery. While it was possible that Trisha and Pricilla had gone for a walk and lost track of time, his gut told him there was more to it. And wherever they were, it had to do with Norton Richards's death and the personal invitation the sheriff had recently extended to Pricilla to help out in the case.

He reached into his pocket for an antacid and sent up a prayer for the safety of the two women. Finding himself smack-dab in the middle of a murder investigation—with Pricilla involved—tended to raise his acid level faster than a bowl of red-hot chili.

While he popped two of the chalky pills into his mouth, snippets of the conversation he'd had with

Pricilla over breakfast replayed in his mind. He couldn't understand why the sheriff, of all people, had asked Pricilla to get involved. The woman had enough determination to find out the truth without encouragement from the law. Deputy Carter might have been impersonal and even rude at times, but at least he was smart enough not to invite Pricilla to become an informant.

Still, whether he was right or not, nothing excused the fact that neither Pricilla nor Trisha had told anyone where they were going. What if something had gone wrong? Pricilla had tried to dismiss his concerns that she was a magnet for trouble, a theory proved by the last two cases she'd gotten involved in. The last thing he wanted to deal with at the moment was another arrest, or kidnapping. . . or something even worse.

Max turned to Nathan. "I have this sick feeling that both your mother's and my daughter's disappearance have something to do with Norton Richards's murder."

Nathan's eyes widened. "Surely you're not serious."

"I'd prefer not to go that direction, but you know your mom. And I know how determined she is at the moment to ensure Clarissa isn't charged with his murder."

Nathan leaned against the railing. "So you think she's off chasing down a batch of clues?"

Max nodded. "That's exactly what I'm thinking. Pricilla's involvement in two murder investigations has given her just enough confidence to think she knows what she's doing, and enough to get her into trouble."

He knew he should give her more credit. Pricilla was intelligent, compassionate, and most of the time, level-headed, but with his heart on the line, he was bound and determined to make sure nothing happened to her.

Max glanced up at Nathan. "There's another reason why I'm worried."

"What's that?"

"Did your mother tell you about her conversation with the sheriff?"

"No. . ."

"For some crazy reason, he's asked her to be his inside source to the investigation. You know, to keep her eyes and ears open for anything she might pick up from either the contestants or the judges."

"His informant?"

"Yep, and while he might be right about the fact that she's in the perfect position, I'm still tempted to go and have a talk with the man."

"Why haven't you?"

"Because you know as well as I do what your mother's reaction would be. Not only would it infuriate her, I'm afraid she'd lose trust in me. She's a grown woman, and for me to go behind her back and discuss the matter. . ."

Nathan shoved his hands into his pockets. "I, for one, think it's a good idea."

"Except she wasn't exactly pleased with my reaction to the request, and I'm afraid if I stepped in and tried to stop her, she'd end up being all the more determined to get involved. Though now I wish I would have. Especially if she's in trouble."

Max squinted against the bright sun as he scanned the area. A man fished alone in a boat in the middle of the lake. Another couple stood at the water's edge, their arms around each other like they were the only people around for miles. Two others trudged along the shoreline. One carried a metal detector. Now there was an idea for a safe hobby for him and Pricilla to get involved in. One that might keep her busy enough to stay out of trouble.

"Who's that?"

Max's attention snapped back to the present at Nathan's question. "Where?"

Nathan was pointing at the pair in the distance with the metal detector. One of them wore rubber boots. That definitely took Pricilla out of the running and Trisha as well. He couldn't see either woman going out in such unsightly apparel.

"I think it's them," Nathan said.

"I don't think so." He adjusted his bifocals. "The last time I saw Pricilla, she was wearing a red short-sleeved sweater."

Nathan shook his head. "I'm positive it's them. Let's go."

Max hurried behind Nathan down the narrow staircase that led to the lake. Anger started to brew. He thought Pricilla had more sense than to take off without telling anyone where she was going, and that went for his daughter as well. Especially after a murder had taken place. How was he supposed to take care of her if he couldn't even keep track of her?

The two women stopped dead in their tracks when they saw the men approaching. Nathan had been right. And both women were soaking wet. Max wasn't sure if he should stay furious or burst out laughing at their appearance.

Then he saw the knife in Trisha's hand. All the worry he'd felt earlier swept back over him. He opened his mouth, but Nathan was the first to find his voice.

"What in the world happened, Trisha?"

Max's daughter avoided both their gazes.

Now it was Max's turn to press the interrogation. "Pricilla?"

"Before you go off losing a bunch of steam, hold on." Pricilla set the metal detector against the ground and jutted her chin toward Trisha. "We were out looking. . .for something. . .and. . ."

The women exchanged guilty glances.

"Looking for what?" Max demanded.

Pricilla drew in a sharp breath. "For the moment that doesn't matter. The bottom line is I think we found the murder weapon."

—

Pricilla caught the worry in the men's expressions. And the anger. Max had warned her earlier that morning not to dash off and get herself in trouble, and from where she stood, soaking wet and claiming to have found the murder weapon. . .well, it definitely looked like trouble.

She curled her fingers tighter around the metal detector. "I really can explain."

"I'm the one who needs to explain." Trisha took a step forward.

"Trisha—" Pricilla started.

"It's okay." Trisha held up her hand. "Your mother did this for me, Nathan. For us."

Nathan shook his head. "I don't understand."

"I lost my engagement ring—"

"You *what*?"

"I know." Tears welled in her eyes. "I've been sick over it. I think I might have lost it yesterday while we were throwing rocks. It was a bit loose and. . ."

Nathan frowned. "Thus the metal detector."

"So this wasn't a quest to solve the murder?" Max asked.

"Not at all, and granted, we aren't certain this is the murder weapon."

"Seems too much of a coincidence to me," Max threw in.

Nathan folded his arms across his chest and shook his head. "So you went off looking for your ring. How in the world could you have fallen in. . .again?"

"I told you I wasn't the outdoor type."

He cocked his head, as if waiting for a more reasonable explanation. "Yes, you did."

"I'm better with computers and running board meetings."

"I know."

Trisha stepped forward to put her arms around his neck. "And you still want to marry me?"

"Well, you do look kind of cute when you're wet."

"Nathan. I am sorry about the ring."

Nathan chuckled as he pulled her into his arms and kissed her firmly on the lips.

"What I want to know is if you are both all right," Max said.

"Yes, we're fine," Pricilla assured him.

"As long as you're okay." Nathan kissed Trisha again. "That's all that really matters."

Pricilla cleared her throat and turned to Max. "So am I off the hook, too?"

"Not so fast." He bridged the gap between them and took her hand. "Something tells me that this won't be the last time you stick your nose into this investigation."

"I told you, I couldn't make any promises."

"Even with a possible murder weapon in your possession—"

"A murder weapon that could clear Clarissa. It's the one hole in their case against her."

"Which would mean there's been a murderer on the loose while you've been tromping through the great outdoors alone." Max's brow furrowed.

"You scared me, Pricilla. I'm not ready to lose you."

She shook her head. "You're not going to."

He leaned down and kissed her, reminding her that love can shoot tingles to your toes whether you're sixteen or sixty-five.

He pulled back and ran his thumb down her cheek, making her wish she didn't look like such a mess. Perhaps there was truth in the old adage that true love was blind. Even dripping wet and wearing rubber boots, the spark still simmered.

"I suppose we need to go find the sheriff now," he said.

"Surely even you can't ignore possible evidence."

Nathan and Trisha trudged up the slope ahead of them, arm in arm. Nathan's cell phone rang, and he reached to answer it.

Max took Pricilla's hand, and they followed the younger couple back toward the lodge. Not only was she going to have to find the sheriff, she was going to have to ask Michelle to take her place for the next segment, something she was quite certain Michelle wouldn't mind. Being in front of the camera seemed to be her thing.

Nathan stopped and snapped his phone shut. "Your

ring isn't the only thing lost."

"What are you talking about?" Trisha said.

"Our travel agent called to confirm the details on the added excursion I requested."

"And. . ."

"Apparently, the hotel has lost our honeymoon reservation."

7

There was something to this Murphy's Law. Pricilla had never believed in bad luck, but she couldn't deny the fact that any plans of a relaxing weekend had been waylaid.

I know You're in control, Lord, but things sure do seem to be spiraling out of control.

She trudged toward the lodge behind the others in the cumbersome rubber boots, feeling every aching muscle in her body. A bruise had formed on her right wrist where she'd hit it against a rock, and her head throbbed. While being young at heart might keep her spirit alive, she now had even more reason for steering clear of rigorous outdoor excursions.

Max slowed down to match her pace while Nathan and Trisha hurried ahead, lost in conversation. A misplaced hotel reservation might justifiably seem insignificant compared to a murder, but Pricilla also knew that didn't take away the irritation of the situation. Another fly in the ointment was not what the couple needed at this point.

She stopped at the tackle shop to return the borrowed boots and metal detector, quickly donning her own sturdy shoes again.

"Are you sure you're okay?" Max reached for her hand as they started walking again.

"A bruise or two, but I'm fine." A glance his direction left her heart beating in that familiar pitter-patter rhythm that only a bout of true love could evoke.

He looked as handsome today as he had the first time

she'd met him, with his broad shoulders and military physique. Friends for decades, she'd never expected anything more, but somehow they'd found it. And now he was even more handsome. His hair had turned gray, giving him a look of maturity, and he still had a trim figure despite his constant craving for sweets.

A wave of guilt washed over her as they continued toward the lodge. She'd looked forward to this weekend as time together for the two of them. Living hundreds of miles apart wasn't easy, and until the wedding, or until Max's house sold, they had no choice but to endure a long-distance relationship.

Maybe it was time to stop focusing on excuses and simply set the wedding date.

But all thoughts of romance fled as Pricilla stopped at the bottom of the stairs leading up to the lodge's restaurant. Michelle perched at the stop of the stairs, clipboard in hand, her displeasure evident.

Pricilla turned to Max. "Michelle's waiting for me, and you know she isn't going to take my late or untidy appearance well."

"Knowing you, you'll find a way to placate her."

Pricilla had exactly fifteen seconds to figure something out. She took the stairs slowly, forcing a smile as she stepped onto the deck.

Michelle wasn't smiling. "Mrs. Crumb. Where in the world have you been?"

Pricilla scrambled to think of something to say that wouldn't completely erase the tiny bit of dignity she had left. A good reputation had always been important to her, and if she wasn't careful, the professionalism and integrity she worked to portray would be lost in an instant.

She combed her fingers through her disheveled hair. "I was involved in a bit of an accident, Michelle. Trisha and I. . .we. . ."

"I can see you've been involved in some sort of recreation." Michelle's lips puckered. "The next round of the competition begins in ten minutes. I'm already down a judge and a contestant and have a second contestant thinking about dropping out because of this morning's fiasco. Now on top of all that, it seems that my emcee has decided to go swimming. This isn't good for publicity, Mrs. Crumb. For the continuity of the show and for the sponsors who wanted the face of. . .of Julia Child, I need you in front of the camera in. . ." She glanced at her watch. ". . .eight and a half minutes."

"I'm very well aware of that." Pricilla clenched her fists beside her. She was also aware of the fact that she'd never be presentable in twice that amount of time.

Trisha held the knife out of sight behind her back. "This is all my fault, really—"

"It's okay, Trisha," Pricilla said. "Go on upstairs and change. I'll be there shortly."

As Nathan and Trisha skirted away with the evidence, Pricilla wondered if it was even possible to soothe Michelle's ruffled feathers. The woman had tunnel vision when it came to her work. Far be it for even a murder investigation to get in the way of her project.

Pricilla decided on another angle. "While I realize that I've put you in an extremely awkward position, don't you think the sponsors would welcome seeing a bit of the woman who has worked so hard to make this contest the success that it is?"

Max cleared his throat beside her. Pricilla avoided

looking at him. There were times when one simply had to pull out all the diplomatic cards available.

"You've done an outstanding job," Pricilla rushed on, "and you deserve some time in the spotlight. This afternoon's opening segment would give you just that. I can't see anyone complaining about that."

"Well, I. . ." Michelle pushed back her highlighted bangs with her fingers. "I suppose no one would mind."

Bingo. Appealing to the woman's vanity had been the right card to play.

Pricilla smiled. "And I promise I'll be ready to go on in time for the next segment."

Michelle checked the schedule she carried. "I'll expect you in front of the camera at two thirty." The frown was back, but Pricilla knew she'd won. The younger woman turned on her high heels. "Don't be late a second time."

With Michelle placated for the moment, Pricilla relaxed. She'd have just enough time to change her clothes, do something to her hair, and grab a quick lunch before resuming her role. Missing one spot was bad enough. Missing the next assigned slot would be unacceptable.

"I'm not sure I trust her."

"What do you mean?" Pricilla walked beside Max across the thick area carpet through the lobby toward the elevator, thankful the lobby was empty for the moment, except for the receptionist who was talking on the phone.

"You told me that when you spoke to Michelle, she admitted to knowing Norton, but that they weren't friends."

Intrigued, Pricilla stopped at the elevator and punched the button. "She seemed quite emphatic on the point, even stating that the man had no friends, only enemies and that he, even beyond the grave, was trying to ruin her career."

"It seems she was quite passionate on the matter." Max folded his arms across his chest. "Why?"

"I don't know if *passionate* is the word, though someone obviously was passionate enough to kill the man."

"Well, I happened to have a chat with Christopher Jeffries while you were out treasure hunting."

"And. . ."

"He emphatically implied that Michelle and Norton were far more than friends at one time."

"Really?" The elevator doors opened, and Pricilla stepped in before Max. "And how would he know something like that?"

Pricilla's interest peaked as Max filled her in on the details of his conversation with Christopher.

"Michelle definitely told me quite the opposite. That they couldn't stand each other." They stepped out of the elevator and walked toward Pricilla's room.

"What is the old saying—opposites attract? They still could have had a romantic encounter."

"Still, it sounds to me as if one of them is lying."

"Maybe, but on the surface I see no reason why Christopher would lie. If you ask me, Michelle has more to hide than her wrinkles."

"Max." She stood at her door, passkey in hand, wondering if there was merit to Max's discovery or if it was nothing more than a thread of gossip.

"We can talk about it later. You change and I'll go save us a table in the restaurant." He leaned down and brushed her lips with his before he walked away, leaving her more to think about than simply a potential murder weapon.

﹏

While the women changed into dry clothes and Nathan battled with the travel agent over their lost reservations, Max called the sheriff, who promised to be at the hotel within the next thirty minutes. With the knife now in a plastic baggie procured from the kitchen, he'd gone back downstairs to reserve a table for five from the perky waitress who asked if he was back for seconds on the pie. He wondered for a moment if he could get by with another slice but then decided against it.

The sheriff arrived five minutes after the women, giving them just enough time to order salads and iced teas. Nathan was still pacing on the deck outside the restaurant, on hold with the travel agent who had booked their honeymoon package.

Max slid the evidence across the table to the sheriff.

The lawman's eyes widened. "Where did you find this?"

Pricilla explained the exact location where they'd found the knife.

The sheriff held the bag up in front of him. "There is, of course, no way to know whether or not this is connected to the case at this point, but if it is indeed the murder weapon, it could punch a hole in the DA's case."

"Exactly," Pricilla said, taking a sip of her water. "Which in turn could exonerate Clarissa."

"Potentially." The sheriff slipped the knife into his briefcase. "Anything else?"

Max paused, wondering if he should mention his conversation with Christopher, but decided against it. At this point the truth was still rather fuzzy.

Pricilla leaned forward, her voice lowered. "So what do we do next?"

Max frowned, pointing at her. "This part of *we* has already been in enough trouble this week, wouldn't you say, Pricilla?"

"Max."

The sheriff shrugged. "I realize your concern, but Pricilla has already been a help to the case."

"So you're convinced Clarissa is innocent?" Pricilla asked.

"Yes," he admitted. He stood up and grabbed his bag. "I appreciate your help, but if you will all excuse me, I'll be in touch."

The lawman slipped out of the restaurant as the waitress served their food.

"I'm surprised you didn't order a slice of the coconut pie," Pricilla said as she reached for the pepper.

He felt his cheeks redden and decided to confess. "I had one earlier when I joined Christopher. Though it was in order to further conversation, of course, and not appear to make it an interrogation session."

"Good try." She took a sip of her water.

Wanting to avoid an argument, he jumped into another subject. "So tell me what you all know about Norton Richards."

"I used to follow his column religiously," Trisha admitted. "You've read it before, haven't you?"

Max cleared his throat. "I can't say that I have, actually."

"He was eccentric," Pricilla began. "He had a temper, and of course, a ruthless pen. His reviews were full of wit, but as you know by now, were also very tough."

"Which gave him a love-hate relationship with the world."

"Exactly," Pricilla continued. "Most restaurants hated him, at least those who didn't receive a good review, but the public loved him, and he became a sort of icon. Good reviews, of course, were coveted, because they brought in business. Bad reviews could crush a business with his trademarked phrase 'the deadly dish' that was given to menu items he didn't like."

"Hmm, 'the deadly dish.'" Max set his fork down and frowned. "Seemed to have been a bit of a prophecy."

He felt a shudder run down his spine. No one had expected the killer review of a deadly dish to turn into murder, but unless they were mistaken, that was exactly what had happened.

8

With Pricilla back to work as the hostess of the contest, Max decided it best to stay away from the samples of gourmet food. As hard as it was to admit, Pricilla did have a point. Fishing and walking down the long hallways of the hotel only went so far to counteract the desserts and high-calorie foods he'd been indulging in this weekend. Besides, he could always make up for anything he missed at supper.

A sense of déjà vu washed over him as he made his way to the small business center adjacent to the hotel's lobby. While he had no illusions of discovering the murderer simply from an online search, anything he could add to the investigation of Norton and his deadly dish was a step closer to getting Pricilla off the case. And his motivation was strong. He'd told her that her involvement with the investigation was sure to lead to trouble, and in less than twenty-four hours, his words had proven true.

It was time to put an end to all of this.

He glanced at his watch. With an hour and a half left in this afternoon's hors d'oeuvre competition, he had just enough time to do a bit of research online. At least Pricilla was safe for now. Surely nothing could happen to her while she stood in front of a television camera.

Armed with a small notebook containing a potential list of suspects, he slid in front of a computer. Besides a twenty-something-year-old wearing headphones while playing an online game, the small room was empty. He grabbed the mouse and clicked on the Internet icon. He'd run background checks from time to time in the military, and while he didn't have nearly the resources he once had, something was better than nothing.

First on his list was one of the judges, Lyle Simpson, owner of an upscale Italian restaurant outside Denver. It didn't take long to find the first round of startling news. Two months ago, Simpson put his restaurant up for sale. He printed out a copy of the article and clicked on another link. Further digging revealed that the former five-star venue was facing bankruptcy. While the notable television personality might be a draw for the competition, apparently the popular chef's business had run amok. He couldn't help but wonder what Michelle would think, knowing that one of her esteemed judges was about to go under financially.

There were other possibilities, of course, that could play into the equation. Gambling, debt, drinking—if Pricilla were here, she would add a tainted review by Norton to the list. Max jotted down a couple more facts, still unconvinced that a restaurant could go under simply because of one of Norton's so-called deadly reviews. Couldn't it just be nothing more than bad management of a once-superior venue? Or maybe it was simply that Lyle was a better chef than businessman.

He maneuvered his way through the contestants, stopping to print out bios that might be applicable, until he came to Michelle Vanderbilt. Max googled the woman's name and scrolled through the links. Because of her possible romantic connection to Norton, Max would have bet his savings account—if he'd been a gambling man—on her involvement in Norton's murder. Two of the articles revealed career triumphs for the woman while implying the fallout of others in the process. Perhaps Norton wasn't the only person who was eager to take down whoever he could on his way up.

He clicked on a third article. Two years ago Michelle was arrested for attacking a colleague. The charges were later dropped because it was a situation of "she said, she said." Nevertheless, it all seemed to be here. A relationship with the victim, history of violence, possible motive because of rocky history with victim. . .

Someone dumped a large wicker bag on the floor and then slid into the chair beside him. Max looked over at Michelle's assistant, Sarah Reynolds. She wore little makeup beyond lip gloss and perhaps some powder. Black slacks, white sweater, hair pulled back in a ponytail. . .

She smiled at him as she clicked on her own Internet icon. "You're Pricilla Crumb's fiancé, aren't you?"

Max returned her smile and nodded.

"I think it's so romantic for an old. . ." She cleared her throat, shoving a piece of gum into her mouth. "For a couple more advanced in years to find love."

"Advanced in years?" His eyes widened at her choice of words. He'd yet to get to the age where he was ready to be rolled into an old folks' home with his teeth in a cup beside him.

In Michelle's presence, Sarah was hardly noticeable. He'd never heard her say more than "yes, ma'am" or "no, ma'am." While her looks might not be on par with a cover model, he had to give her some credit. She must have a lot of discipline to put up with her demanding boss.

Max closed out the page and grabbed his papers from the printer. He didn't want Sarah to know that he was researching her boss. Still, he might as well take advantage of the opportunity. Anyone working for the magazine would have come in contact with Norton at some point.

"So you're the photographer for this weekend's activities," he threw out.

"Technically, no. I'm actually more of a girl Friday. You know. The ever-faithful and efficient assistant who's taken for granted." The girl's glossy lips widened as she laughed. "Of course, you would know what a girl Friday means. My mom always said I'm too old for my age."

Max raised his brows. *Ouch.* Another reminder of his age.

"I mean the age thing in all due respect, of course." A dreamy look crossed her face as she chomped on her gum. "I should have been born fifty years earlier, when they had real actors like Cary Grant and Clark Gable. The movie *His Girl Friday* has always been one of my favorites. You know, with Cary Grant and Rosalind Russell. Movie stars don't come like him anymore, do they? Though perhaps the movie became like a self-fulfilling prophecy with me becoming a girl Friday. Still, I like a man who's mature and a bit older, like you."

A bit older? Max swallowed hard. He had to be more than thirty years the girl's senior. Avoiding her pensive gaze, he wondered how she could breathe while talking so much. Apparently he hadn't learned his lesson last time about the pitfalls of trying to interview younger—much younger—women. In the first murder investigation Pricilla had dragged him into, he'd offered to interview one of the suspects and then had to leave the room, running like a coon with his tail on fire from the young woman's blatant pursuit.

No. He brushed the ridiculous thought aside. He was

simply on edge and reading things into the situation.

"Of course I remember Cary Grant," he started. "Not that I knew him personally, as he was born several decades before I was. . ." Here he went again. It was definitely time to change the subject. Sarah seemed hungry for attention, a definite advantage when extracting information from a source. "So what's your take on the murder?"

"If the rumors are true, that the authorities think Clarissa might be innocent. . ." She leaned forward and lowered her voice. "The top of my list is Violet Peterson."

Max raised his brow. He'd yet to google this judge and restaurant owner.

"What do you know about her?"

"A bit of inside info from my job." She looked around the room. Besides the guy playing videos and wearing headphones, the room was still empty.

"It's a recipe for disaster if you ask me." She blew a bubble and then sucked it back in. "Michelle would fire me if she saw me chewing gum."

"What's a recipe for disaster?" he asked, urging her to continue.

"Violet owns this swanky French restaurant. You know the kind you wouldn't dare go into without a suit and tie and that I couldn't afford to go into on the salary the magazine pays me. Anyway, Norton wrote a scandalous review last year that claimed her Coquille St. Jacques and stuffed mushrooms tasted worse than an overcooked microwave dinner. It was so lethal, in fact, that Violet's lawyers served Norton legal papers claiming malice and defamation."

"Did anything come of it?"

"Not yet."

Max tapped his fingers against the desk. "Maybe it's just me, but I have a hard time believing that Norton had that much influence over people. Shutting down restaurants, owners filing for bankruptcy. . .if that were true, then half the restaurants in the country would be out of business simply because Norton didn't like their special of the day or thought there was too much salt in the soufflé."

Sarah crossed her legs, still chomping on her gum. "Look at Elvis and the Beatles, for example."

"Please don't tell me that you're comparing Norton Richards to those music legends."

"Of course not. They had real talent, but that doesn't change the fact that our society will take almost anyone and make them into an icon if they fit the need for the moment."

"So Norton appealed to people's need for what? Finding the best hamburger in town?"

She shook her head. "You definitely didn't know Norton."

"What do you mean?"

"Despite the man's gruff exterior, he really did know what he was talking about. Yes, his words could cut worse than a butcher knife, but for a top-rated review, he expected a lot and thrived on honesty no matter how brutal it might be. His reviews gave some restaurants the well-deserved publicity they needed to boost their clientele, as well."

"So you knew him?"

"You could say that." Sarah's laugh came out more like a snort.

"Meaning. . ."

"Norton Richards didn't have time for people like me.

I'm too low on the ladder to be a threat and not high enough to help his career."

"You shouldn't be so hard on yourself."

"Oh, I've never minded flying under the radar. It's allowed me to get information I wouldn't otherwise be able to." She blew another bubble and let it pop. "I'm not naive enough to think I'll make it big in this industry. Fashion, food, and starting the latest craze require finesse. To get anywhere you need to either have that certain charisma or the ability to climb over people on your way to the top."

Like Michelle and Norton?

"So how did you get to know Norton?"

"I worked for him for five years before I was hired by *Food Style* magazine."

"You worked for him?" Max hadn't expected this.

"Norton doesn't do much speaking anymore. . .well, before he died he didn't. . .but besides his restaurant reviews, he used to do speaking engagements, talk shows, radio slots, and the like."

"So you were his assistant."

"Yeah." Sarah punched in an Internet address, pausing until her e-mail service popped up. "But I didn't get a degree in journalism to spend the rest of my life making appointments for other people and making sure their electric bills get paid. That's why I'm getting out."

Max quirked his left eyebrow. "Getting out?"

"I probably shouldn't tell you this, but I've written a book." She turned back to him and leaned forward. "It's a biography of sorts. Unauthorized and currently in the middle of a bidding war with two big New York publishing houses."

Murder aside, the young woman had his curiosity piqued.

She popped her gum. "It's the truth behind a certain icon of the food industry."

Now she really had his attention. "And who would that be?"

Sarah smiled. "Norton Richards."

—

Max crossed the lobby following the afternoon's competition, still unsure whether he should add Sarah Reynolds to the list of suspects or take her off. She didn't seem to hold animosity toward the man, but dead, Norton would have no rights of privacy, giving Sarah the freedom to write what she wanted. The advance from a bidding war could bring in a hefty amount. What if Norton had tried to stop the unauthorized book from being published? But surely if she'd killed Norton she wouldn't have wanted the information about the book to leak out. On the other hand, such information was bound to come out eventually, and maybe she thought it better to make it public before the police did.

He stopped at the Silvermist Café, wanting to make sure he'd remembered everything. With no competition during the dinner hour, he'd planned a romantic meal for Pricilla on the back deck overlooking the lake. Arriving early, he was assured that his request for a private table and flowers had been filled.

Pricilla entered the dining room five minutes behind him, wearing a deep purple jacket with black slacks. He caught her smile. Time had only managed to make her more beautiful to him. Any regrets of leaving his home in New Mexico to be with her had long since vanished.

Watching her walk across the room toward him, he was reminded that it was time to set a wedding date. He wasn't willing to wait indefinitely for all the details of selling houses and moving to be worked out. At his age, every day was a gift. A gift he intended to share with her. Norton's death had reminded him just how fleeting life really was.

He shoved any thoughts of the investigation aside. Everything he'd learned this afternoon had only managed to muddy the waters. For now he'd keep the latest details of the case to himself and focus on Pricilla, knowing she'd have her own theories to share with him anyway.

"You look beautiful." He took her hands and kissed her briefly on the lips.

Her smile widened. "After your dinner invitation, I decided I should change out of the rubber boots and look for something a bit more appealing."

"Whatever you did worked." He wrapped his arm around her waist, anticipating a quiet hour together. "There's something we need to talk about."

"Is everything all right?"

"Everything is fine," he said, leading her to the table the servers had set for them near the edge of the deck. Late afternoon rays of sunlight scattered across the lake, leaving a glowing hue above the mountains.

"So what did you do during this afternoon's competition?"

He pulled back her chair, wondering how much he should tell her. "A little research. . ."

"Research?"

He'd said the wrong thing, but he wasn't going to let her steer him that direction. Not yet, anyway. He took his seat across from her. "Nothing life-shattering. I'll tell you later about that. First things first. I haven't had enough of you to myself, and for now, I only want to focus on us."

The waitress set down two bowls in front of them. He'd ordered everything ahead of time, from the starter course to the butterflied shrimp and savory rice for the main course, to the dessert.

Pricilla frowned when she saw the creamed asparagus soup.

"It's their special of the day, with top reviews from the customers I interviewed."

She laughed, but from her expression, she wasn't buying into his reasoning.

"You're right." She held up her hand. "I'm not saying a word. This evening's about us, and speaking of us, then, I think it's time we set a date."

"For the wedding?"

"If we don't, the planning stage could go on forever. And I'm not nearly as young as I used to be."

He couldn't help but smile. His thoughts exactly. She was smiling again, too. Perhaps wedding talk would be enough of a distraction for him to get away with the high-cholesterol cheesecake he'd ordered for dessert.

⁓

Pricilla took the last bite of her cheesecake and pushed the plate aside. She'd regret finishing the slice later, especially after the huge meal Max had ordered for them, but for now, she was enjoying every minute of the evening. In the past hour, they'd settled on a date for the wedding, discussed where they would live afterward, and how much they were anticipating their children's wedding.

And not even a mention of the murder, for which she was grateful. All she had to do now was check to ensure that a December wedding didn't conflict with her friends' holiday social calendars or her work commitments at the lodge. In a few short months, she'd be Mrs. Max Summers.

She squeezed her eyes shut, picturing the quiet ceremony inside Nathan's lodge with a few select friends and family. Poinsettias for decoration, a violin quartet playing in the background. . .simple, yet elegant.

"Pricilla?"

Her eyes popped open. "Sorry. I was daydreaming about the wedding."

"We don't have to wait that long."

She felt her cheeks redden at his smile. "There's so much to do, and December is only three months away," she began.

He took a sip of his coffee. "I thought we were going to keep things small and intimate."

The word *elope* crossed her mind again. Maybe he was right. Why wait until December? All they had to do was make sure Nathan and Trisha were able to tie the knot. Then they'd be free to tie their own nuptials.

"Let's finalize the details of our wedding after Trisha and Nathan's." She still wanted to deal with the question that had been nagging at her. "You told me you did some research this afternoon."

The murder investigation might have been an off-topic subject for the last hour, but if Max had stumbled across anything important, she needed to know.

"I'll give you five minutes if you promise to go on a walk with me after supper with no mention of the case. I finally have you to myself, and the sky is clear, the stars bright—"

"Okay." Pricilla laughed as he signaled the waitress for coffee refills. There was something about being in love that made her giddy. "You don't have to convince me."

"Well, I'm not sure how much the sheriff knows, or how much he needs to know, but to put it briefly, I had an interesting conversation with Sarah."

"Michelle's assistant?"

The waitress came by with a pot of coffee and filled their cups before they continued their conversation. "Apparently she used to work for Norton."

"Really?" Max had her attention now. She hadn't expected this twist.

"But that's not all. She's just finished an unauthorized manuscript of Norton's life."

Pricilla's head began to spin as he went on to give her the details of their conversation. "Talk about fuel for the fire."

"One that's growing out of control by the minute." Max grabbed a thin stack of folded papers from his jacket pocket. "I don't know if these will help, but I did a bit of my own research today and printed out some bios of most of the main suspects."

"This is great." She set down the sugar spoon for her coffee and began thumbing through the papers. "So all we need to find out now is which suspect was willing to take the matter into his own hands by killing Norton. What about—"

"Wait a minute." Max grasped her hands, shooting a tingling sensation through her that went all the way to her toes. "I believe your five minutes are up."

9

The question still haunted Pricilla when she awoke the next morning. While the list of viable suspects grew by the hour, only one person had struck the fatal blow that killed Norton. So if Clarissa wasn't the perpetrator, then who was?

She rolled over in the queen-sized bed and shoved off the covers, wishing she could go back to sleep instead of facing another day in front of the cameras. She didn't have to look into the mirror to know that, with the stress of the last two days, her crow's-feet had multiplied, and the circles beneath her eyes darkened. In a world that thrived on youth and beauty, whose idea had it been to stick her in front of the camera?

And what had she been thinking when she said yes?

Pricilla shoved on her slippers and yawned. At least she'd have a chance to speak to Clarissa today. The poor girl's parents—if they even knew yet about the incarceration—must be frantic with worry. It hadn't been so long ago when Pricilla had feared that Deputy Carter was going to drag Nathan into custody during the investigation into Reggie Pierce's murder.

Trisha peeked up from the other side of her bed. "Did I wake you?"

"Trisha?" Pricilla slipped her glasses on and took a second look. "What on earth are you doing on the floor?"

Trisha disappeared behind the thick rose-colored comforter again. "I'm looking for my ring."

"I thought you lost it near the lake."

"I think I did, but I'm not ready to give up." She rounded the foot of the bed on her hands and knees, stopping in front of the dresser. "And I'm still not completely dismissing the possibility that it's in this room."

Pricilla glanced down at the carpet below her. She loved her future daughter-in-law, but there was no way she was going to attempt a search under her bed. Days of flexibility and litheness had ended more than a decade ago when she gave up yoga, and the last place she wanted to find herself was stuck in some precarious position on the floor.

Instead, she slid her robe on and rotated her neck to work out the kinks of sleeping on a too-soft bed. "Did you sleep all right?"

"Besides dreaming that the lake had turned into some huge monster with long fangs?" Trisha peered up at Pricilla beneath a row of bangs. "I still can't believe I lost the ring."

"There's still a chance it might show up."

"Maybe." Trisha dragged a chair across the floor and crawled into the empty spot behind it. "I'm afraid that even if I did drop it in here, more than likely the maid vacuumed it up."

Pricilla sensed the desperation in her voice and searched for a word of encouragement. "I doubt most maids take the time to clean all those hard-to-get spots. You know how most workers are these days."

Trisha was still inching her fingers along the floorboards of the far wall when Pricilla entered the bathroom to brush her teeth and wash her face. At some point, Trisha was going to have to face the fact that the ring was likely lost for good. That is, if the young woman's instincts were right and it had sunk to the bottom of the lake.

After brushing her teeth, Pricilla squeezed a dab of cleanser onto her hands, ran them under the water, and began her morning ritual of attempting to erase the years—a feat that so far had never been accomplished. "So what did you and Nathan do for supper last night?"

"We ended up eating with J. J. Rhymes, one of the judges, and I have to tell you, that man's a born comedian."

"Really?" Pricilla turned off the water and stepped back into the room. While J.J. was on her list of suspects to interview, she'd not yet found the opportunity to talk to the rotund restaurant owner. "What is he like?"

"For starters, he's the only person I've met so far who doesn't seem to have a bone to pick with Norton." Trisha shoved back the heavy drapes and searched along the floorboard beneath the window. "Quite the opposite, actually. Apparently they knew each other from college."

"Really?" Pricilla dabbed her face with one of the plush white towels all hotels seemed to own, wondering if the relationship between Norton and Rhymes could have any relevance to the case. "So they were friends?"

Trisha made her way toward the adjacent wall. "It didn't sound as if they celebrated Christmas or birthdays together, but J.J. claims that his business quadrupled after a five-star review from Norton this past year. Business, apparently, has never been so good."

Certainly didn't sound like a motive for murder, but if Pricilla had learned anything at all during the past two investigations she'd been involved in, it was that most people have hidden agendas. What one saw on the outside was often meant to hide the truth hovering beneath the surface, and at this point, she wasn't yet ready to dismiss anyone except Clarissa as a suspect.

Trisha stood, hands on her hips, eyeing the corner of the room like a surveyor. "He also claimed that a bad review from Norton was most always justly deserved."

"Now that's a first." Pricilla set the towel down and reached for her jar of face cream. "Everyone I've talked to insisted that the man's reviews were unfair. . .or worse. Of course, these were people who found themselves recipients of Norton's 'deadly dish' reviews. The man had to garner fans when he gave out good reviews."

"J.J. received a five-star, the highest award from Norton, so it's no wonder he's not complaining."

Pricilla added an extra layer of cream under her eyes. J.J.'s take on Norton, while not incriminating, was definitely interesting. "Did he happen to give his opinion on the murder?"

"We briefly touched on the subject. He seemed glad that Clarissa was behind bars. When I told him that the authorities had some questions as to her guilt, he reiterated that he thought the government spent far too much time trying to determine people's guilt when the evidence was clear, and in this case at least, he didn't see the need to search any further."

Words from a guilty conscious? Perhaps relief that a scapegoat now sat behind bars? Pricilla frowned. No. That was definitely stretching the situation. Still, his support for the victim did stand out in a murky sea of dislike for Norton. At this point in the investigation, anyone claiming the man was anything but a low-down weasel made an investigator stand up and take note. Time would tell whether or not there was merit to Trisha's observation.

The closet door flew open with a *thud*. Pricilla peeked out of the bathroom with a bottle of liquid base in one hand and a sponge in the other. Trisha had thrown open the closet doors and was now frantically searching the pockets of each article of clothing that was hung up.

"Trisha. . ."

"It's got to be here somewhere. I've searched under the beds, behind the dresser, along the floorboards. . ."

Pricilla set down her makeup and moved to put her hands on Trisha's shoulders. "You'll never find it this way."

Trisha sat down on the bed and combed her fingers through her hair. "I've lost it, haven't I? And I'm not talking just about the ring."

Pricilla sat down beside her. "Everything you're feeling is perfectly normal, but I have to tell you one thing."

Trisha drew her legs up toward her chest and stared at Pricilla with red-rimmed eyes. "What's that?"

"In the end none of this really matters. None of the wedding mishaps. Not even the lost ring."

Trisha's eyes widened. "But this is my wedding. The day I've dreamed of since I was seven."

"Which is exactly my point." Pricilla rushed on to clarify. "Yes, the wedding dress, honeymoon, and ring are important, but what really matters is that you and Nathan work to make yours a marriage that lasts forever. Everyone wants a spectacular wedding. Very few, it seems, want a marriage that works the way God planned."

Trisha wiped her face with the backs of her hands and laughed. "I suppose I have been a bit preoccupied with wedding details lately. I've probably been driving Nathan crazy."

"Nathan loves you."

"I know."

A woman's loud voice rose in volume from outside her room. Michelle? Sarah? She couldn't be sure. "Have you looked inside the dresser?"

"Yes."

"Under the nightstands?"

"Yes—"

A sharp knock rapped at the door, interrupting their conversation.

Pricilla tightened her robe around her waist and hurried to answer it. "Now who could that be?"

Riley stood in the doorway all smiles, looking far too perky for seven in the morning.

"Riley, I—"

"I know I should have called," she interrupted, her smile never failing. "Is Trisha here?"

"Yes." Pricilla stepped aside, and the young woman swept into the room like a tornado.

"I found it."

"You found it?" Trisha shook her head. "Found what?"

Riley dug into her front pocket and held up a ring. Trisha's ring. Pricilla's jaw fell open. Trisha stood beside her speechless as Riley pressed the missing ring into the palm of her hand.

"I don't understand."

"I got up early this morning to work on your dress and found it caught in the hem. It must have gotten wedged on the fabric and fallen off while I was altering it."

"I just can't believe it. . .thank you."

Riley laughed, her red hair bouncing over her eyes. "When I found it amidst the piles of fabric, I knew you must have been frantic, so I rushed right over here."

Trisha slid the ring on her finger and then gave Riley an energetic hug. "I can't thank you enough. And to think of all the trouble I've gotten myself into trying to find it."

"Trouble?"

Pricilla laughed. "You don't want to know."

Trisha held up her hand and stared at the diamond. "I really don't know how to thank you, Riley."

"It's not a problem. I know you must be so relieved."

Pricilla pulled a pressed suit jacket from the closet and turned to the girls. "Why don't the two of you join Max and me for breakfast downstairs?"

Riley shook her head. "Normally I'd jump at the chance, but I've got a wedding dress to finish."

"And I've got to find Nathan and tell him the news."

Pricilla pressed the outfit against her before glancing at her watch. "I'm supposed to meet him in fifteen minutes, which doesn't give me near enough time to put myself together."

Twenty minutes later Pricilla left the room, noting that Trisha couldn't keep her eyes off her ring. At least she had one good reason to smile again despite the seemingly sabotaged wedding.

Not wanting to be later than she already was, Pricilla hurried down the hall outside her room. Halfway down the narrow corridor, someone bounded out of one of the rooms behind her. She turned and cocked her head in order to see the face beneath the pile of clothes the person carried. "Sarah?"

"Mrs. Crumb. Good morning." Sarah moved a jacket aside and shot her a sheepish smile. The young woman was loaded down with clothes, books, and other paraphernalia presumably necessary for today's competition. "Michelle just called me up with a list of things she needs downstairs, including two complete changes of clothes."

"What in the world happened?"

"For starters, someone dumped a glass of grape juice down the front of her suit, and she has a meeting with the hotel manager in five minutes."

A notebook slipped from Sarah's hands, landing at Pricilla's feet. "Why don't you let me help?"

"I would appreciate it." Sarah handed Pricilla the pile of clothes and reached down to pick up the notebook. "I knew it was going to be one of those days when Charlie called before seven."

"Who's Charlie?"

Sarah repositioned the stack of books before heading down the hall again toward the elevator. "Michelle's fiancé. She tends to get a bit animated when she talks to him, especially when he doesn't do what she wants."

"So that's the ruckus I heard while I was getting dressed."

Sarah nodded. "Charlie was supposed to be here for the contest, but now he says he won't make it because he's got some gig his band has to play at."

Pricilla hurried to keep up with the younger woman. "Your job gives you the inside scoop into all kinds of things, doesn't it?"

"Yes, but too often it's information I could do without." Sarah shifted the camera strap higher up on her shoulder.

Pricilla decided to skip any follow-up on that comment. "Why the extra outfit for Michelle?"

"Just in case she needs to change quickly again. She's

always been paranoid about looking just right."

"A girl Friday, I believe Max called you."

"Photographer, secretary, gopher. . .and that's just for starters." Sarah laughed, but her smile quickly faded. "I bet Mr. Summers told you about my book, too, didn't he?"

Pricilla pressed her lips together, wondering how much she wanted to admit to knowing. Surely it couldn't hurt, and if anything, she might be able to drag out more information from the girl. "Yes, he did."

"I probably shouldn't have told anyone. I realized that my confession made me look a bit. . .guilty?"

"In what way?" Pricilla asked.

Sarah stopped at the elevator and punched the DOWN button. "It won't take people long to presume that with Norton's death, I stand to make a substantial amount of money on my book, which gives me motivation. You know how death always skyrockets sales. But the truth is, writing someone's secrets isn't the same as killing someone."

Pricilla agreed with the girl's logic, but she also knew that Sarah was right about people's presumptions. If word about the book leaked out, it would definitely look suspicious. "While that might be true, I think you need to consider telling the sheriff. He'll take it better hearing it from you than hearing it elsewhere as a rumor."

"I suppose you're right. If it wasn't for the sheriff's orders to stick around, I'd be gone. Michelle made me so angry yesterday, I threatened to quit. Somehow she made me promise to stay. For now, anyway."

"Max said you are planning to quit as soon as the book deal goes through?"

"And not a moment later."

The elevator doors finally slid open. Pricilla stepped into the empty elevator behind Sarah.

"Thanks so much for helping. I couldn't have done it without you."

The elevator door clicked shut. While that probably wasn't true, Pricilla decided to take advantage of the girl's gratitude. Hopefully Sarah wouldn't regret her candid conversation. "I've heard rumors that Michelle had once been romantically involved with Norton."

"Very briefly, but yes. It's a fact I've been debating whether or not to tell the authorities. As much as Michelle drives me crazy, I'd never want to see her get into trouble. They had this love-hate relationship, though honestly, I think the bottom line was that Michelle wanted to stay on his good side. The exclusive interviews and restaurant critiques he did for the magazine always boosted readership and made Michelle look good."

"Did something go sour between them?"

"A couple months ago, rumors began circulating that the popular column Michelle had been trying to get was going to be given to Norton. Michelle's always wanted her own syndicated column, and this one had the potential to reach millions."

Pricilla whistled as the elevator shuddered to a stop. Michelle's motivation to get rid of Norton had just doubled.

"And there is one other thing."

Pricilla pushed the CLOSE DOOR button before the elevator doors could open. "What's that?"

"I really don't want Michelle to get into trouble, but. . ." Sarah hesitated. "The night Norton died, he'd called Michelle's room, and after five minutes or so of fighting, Michelle left the room in a huff. I only know this because I was in her room going over the next day's schedule with her."

"Did she leave to go and see Norton?" Pricilla asked.

"That I don't know. But I do know that she left around ten and didn't return until just after midnight."

"Sounds pretty suspicious to me."

"Maybe, but the truth is, as much as the woman drives me crazy, I can't see her murdering anyone."

"Given the right circumstances, one never knows."

Pricilla was still mulling over her latest bit of information when the sheriff flagged her down in the lobby.

"I see I'm not the only one up and about early." The sheriff hurried across the room. "Any news for me?"

"A few tidbits that might interest you."

"As in. . ."

"Michelle had a fight with Norton the night of the murder."

The sheriff rubbed his chin. "She should have told me. That's quite an oversight on her part."

"Yes, she should have."

He glanced at his watch. "Are you still planning to visit Clarissa today?"

"I have a two-hour lunch break starting at noon. Max was planning to drive me into town then."

"Good." He nodded his head and tugged on the edge of his jacket. "I'm meeting with Miss Vanderbilt now— and I'll be sure and ask her about the fight she had with Norton—then I'm heading back to the station with some information."

"Wait, Sheriff." Pricilla wasn't letting him go yet.

"What kind of information?"

The sheriff glanced around the lobby. Besides the front-desk clerk, the room was empty. Still, he leaned forward and lowered his voice. "We just finished inventorying Clarissa's kitchen."

Pricilla's brow furrowed. From the look on the sheriff's face, it was clear that whatever they'd found, it wasn't good.

"There was one thing missing, but please don't repeat it, as this kind of evidence will end up being crucial to the case."

Pricilla's frown deepened. He was hedging around his answers. It was time to be more direct. "What was missing?"

"A nine-inch knife, identical to the one you found in the lake."

Pricilla tapped her hands against the table and waited beside Max for Clarissa to enter the visiting room. She didn't want to worry about the sheriff's announcement concerning the missing knife because, the truth was, anyone could have lifted it from Clarissa's kitchen. But that did little to stop her apprehension. At least the young woman's parents had finally been contacted and were on their way to Colorado. Until they arrived, Pricilla hoped to be a familiar face that could ease some of Clarissa's fears.

One of the deputies opened the door to the small, square room that held nothing more besides tables and chairs for meetings between the prisoners and their families and friends. Clarissa hesitated briefly in the doorway and then entered.

"Mrs. Crumb. I can't thank you enough for coming." She crossed the room and collapsed into the chair across from them.

Her face was pale and her features strained. Whatever the outcome of the case, this experience would change her forever.

"I'm sorry you've had to go through this." Pricilla reached out and squeezed Clarissa's hands. "How are you?"

"Numb. . .worried. . .terrified." The young woman wiped away a tear.

Pricilla nodded to Max. "You remember meeting Max Summers the opening night of the contest."

"Yes, of course, though it seems like a hundred years

ago." Clarissa toyed with the end of her ponytail. "It's nice to see you again, Mr. Summers."

"Please call me Max. It's good to see you again as well, though I'm sorry it's not under better circumstances. Pricilla told me about you. All good things."

Clarissa's gaze dropped to the table. "I bet she never imagined having to add my arrest to her repertoire of stories."

Pricilla caught the bitterness in her voice. "Clarissa—"

"I didn't do it, Mrs. Crumb." Clarissa pulled away her hand and tensed her jaw. "I didn't kill Mr. Richards."

"I know, sweetie. That's why we're here."

Her eyes widened. "So you really believe me?"

"I've known you since you were five. I realize that people change and that it's been awhile since I've seen you, but yes. I believe you. You have too much of a heart for people to hurt anyone."

Clarissa's frown deepened. "Try convincing the sheriff of that."

"He wants to help you. It's his job to ensure that the truth is known. And I honestly believe he's doing everything in his power to do just that."

She knotted her fingers together. "But you'll help me, too?"

Max chuckled. "She's already on the case. Pricilla has spent the past forty-eight hours trying to find anything that might lead to who killed Norton."

"Really?" Clarissa's lips curled into a half smile, but even that couldn't erase her hollow expression.

"Really. You're in good hands."

Pricilla felt her cheeks redden as she glanced at Max, knowing it took a lot for him to admit she was involved when he preferred her anywhere else but knee-deep in the middle of a murder mystery.

Clarissa's eyes brightened slightly. "So what have you found out so far?"

Pricilla didn't want to see the light in the young woman's eyes dim again, but everything she had at the moment was inconclusive. She had to start somewhere. "What I've learned is that half of the people involved in the contest had a grudge against Norton. The hardest part isn't going to be finding someone with a motive. It's going to be finding the right motive."

"I can believe that." Clarissa groaned. "I heard a number of the contestants griping when they heard Norton was going to be one of the judges."

"Something that doesn't surprise me at all." Pricilla pulled out her notebook, ready to get to work. "First off, I understand you have a lawyer, right?"

Clarissa nodded. "He's an old family friend who flew in from Seattle yesterday."

"Good. Now you know I want to help in any way I can, but I need you to tell me everything. And I need it to be the truth."

"Okay." Clarissa nodded.

Pricilla tapped her pen against her notebook. "Had you met Norton before this weekend?"

"No. Well, not in person, that is."

Pricilla glanced at Max who looked as intrigued with the conversation as she was. "What do you mean?"

Clarissa rubbed her fingers together. "About two years ago, Norton wrote a review for the restaurant I was working at."

"You were working the night he ate there?"

"Yes. I was a sous-chef, working for Jake Filbert at the time."

"I've heard of him."

"He's a wonderful chef, and Norton's review was unwarranted."

"I've heard that while his reviews could be brutal, they were also honest."

"There was nothing honest about this review. Norton complained unendingly about the bland appetizers, tasteless main course, and heavy dessert. Not a word he said was true."

Pricilla pressed her lips together. "Do you think your loyalty to the restaurant could have made your reaction a bit biased?"

Clarissa shook her head. "I believe Norton had a personal vendetta against Jake."

"Why?"

"Jake and Norton went to school together twenty-odd years ago, and they both had dreams to make it big in the industry as chefs. The year they graduated, Jake was admitted into one of Europe's most prestigious cooking schools. Norton wasn't accepted. According to some, he never got over the blow. In the end, Norton found greater success, but grudges can run deep."

"Do you have any proof that Norton meant the review as revenge?" Pricilla asked while scribbling a few notes. There was no use interviewing people if she forgot all the details tomorrow.

"Unfortunately, no. The only thing I could do was write a letter to the editor of the newspaper, but all my efforts ended up backfiring in the end."

"What do you mean?"

"Jake decided that my letter added to the bad publicity and used it as an excuse to fire me."

"Despite his problems with Norton?"

"I tried to ask Jake, but he refused to talk about it. At that point, anything I said would be nothing more than a pile of accusations that I can't substantiate."

"So what happened after you got fired?"

"I found another position eventually, but the damage had been done, especially with my name mentioned in Norton's write-up. I was lucky to have a chance to even participate in the contest, but now, after being arrested for murder. . .well. . .I probably won't be able to find work flipping hamburgers. So much for the chance of winning a scholarship and starting afresh."

Pricilla set down her notebook. Why was it that there were always more questions than answers? "So you saw this contest as a chance to escape from the past and move ahead?"

"Exactly."

"How much does the sheriff know about all of this?"

"He knows about my letter to the editor and my being fired. It seems as if the entire legal system is trying to use the incident as a motive for murder." Clarissa winced. "Which I suppose I can't blame them for. I know it looks bad, but on the other hand this was two years ago. If I'd wanted to knock the guy off, wouldn't I have done it a long time ago?"

"Maybe, but in the end, all it really proves is that you had a bone to pick with Norton like all the rest of them. It doesn't mean you killed him." Pricilla glanced at her notes. She needed more. "What about the other contestants? Do you know of other motives any of them might have?"

Clarissa's laugh rang hollow. "No one was thrilled to have Norton on the panel of judges, but that doesn't mean they killed him. Myself included."

Max shook his head. "Well, someone killed him."

"And that someone is on the loose." Clarissa shuddered. "I've got to get out of here, but they won't let me go until they get enough evidence to arrest someone else."

"Half the people at that contest have a motive," Pricilla said.

Max leaned back and shook his head. "How in the world could one man have made so many enemies?"

"Greed. . .selfishness. . .pride. . .you name it. Though you have to give the guy some credit. He was the top in his field, and most people took his reviews seriously." Clarissa clasped her hands in front of her. "The question is, what do we do now?"

Pricilla wished she had a more concrete strategy. For now, all she could do was continue keeping her eyes and ears open. "I'll keep interviewing the other contestants and trying to find out as much information as I can. At some point, someone will slip. In fact, we've already found a few discrepancies in several stories. Now it's a matter of sorting through them and finding out which are actually relevant to the case. In the meantime, I'd say that the biggest hole in the case against you is the problem of the missing murder weapon. Trisha and I found a knife in the lake that more than likely is the murder weapon."

"In the lake?" Clarissa's eyes widened.

"It's a long story." Pricilla's gaze shifted to Max, but he was staring straight ahead, making her wonder if he was avoiding her gaze because he was still unhappy about her jaunt in the lake or if he was simply trying not to laugh over the way she'd emerged looking more like a drowned rat than Sherlock Holmes. She cleared her throat. "The bottom line is that you couldn't have been two places at once."

"You're talking about the knife they discovered missing from my kitchen?"

Pricilla nodded. "Just because it was from your kitchen doesn't prove you took it. We all know that while access to the kitchens was supposed to be restricted, it wouldn't have been difficult. And for one of the other contestants, it would have been a snap."

"You keep talking about the contestants. Have you thought about one of the judges, someone from the audience, or even the hotel staff for that matter?"

"At this point I'd say it could be anyone."

Clarissa lowered her chin and stared at the table. "But in the end, I was the one standing over Mr. Richards's body. That's the kind of evidence no one can ignore."

"Maybe, but if that knife proves to be the murder weapon, they will have to release you. How could the murderer be found standing over the victim and the weapon be half a mile away at the same time? The entire scenario is impossible."

"Maybe."

Pricilla felt as if she were grasping for straws and didn't like it. "There are no *maybes* about it. And we'll prove it."

"I do appreciate your help, Mrs. Crumb." Clarissa stood to leave. "If there is anything. . .anything at all that I can do, please tell me."

"You just keep praying that this will all be over soon."

"I hope so."

"Mark my words."

The deputy entered the room. Their time with Clarissa might be over, but Pricilla was far from finished with her investigation.

Once outside, she slid into the front seat beside Max and leaned back, the fatigue of the past few days washing over her like a bad dream.

Max started the engine and eased out of the parking lot into the light traffic that filtered down Main Street. "So what do you think? Do you still believe she's innocent?"

"Without a doubt, though our talk with her did manage to raise more questions than it answered. First of all, I want to know more about Jake Filbert, Clarissa's old boss. Sounds to me as if the man had a reason to have a vendetta against Norton."

"Seems pretty straightforward to me. Norton wrote a bad review because he was jealous of Jake, Clarissa wrote a letter, and Jake fired her for writing it—probably she didn't clear it with him first. Seems nothing more to me than another red herring and not an actual clue into Norton's death."

"I suppose you have a point."

"I personally think we should stick to those who are actually here at the contest."

Pricilla smiled despite the heavy fatigue she felt. He'd said "we." She liked the sound of that. She glanced at Max's profile and wondered how she'd ever thought that she was too old to fall in love again. While love might have a few extra complications the second time around, it was still worth it.

Max braked at the stoplight and tapped his fingers against the steering wheel. "Do you mind if we run by the pharmacy on the way back to the lodge?"

"Of course not." Pricilla noted the sign in the next block flashing LINDA'S DRUGSTORE and felt a ping of worry strike. "Are you all right?"

Max muttered something under his breath as he pulled through the intersection.

"What did you say?"

"Antacids." He gripped the steering wheel and avoided her gaze. "I need some more antacids."

"Antacids?" Pricilla started to shoot him an I-told-you-so glare but stopped. While the man had insisted on indulging in every rich, creamy, and fattening item on the menu the past two days, he'd also managed to make it clear at the sheriff's office that he was on her side. Perhaps he deserved a bit of leeway after all.

She nodded. "Of course we can stop. We have time."

Max pulled into the parking lot and parked. Pricilla hurried with him into the store, wondering how many other people staying for the contest had dropped into the same store for a bottle of antacids because of all the rich foods. The small store had four or five neatly arranged aisles boasting everything from first aid products, over-the-counter medicines, and a variety of health aids. Pricilla stopped and pulled Max behind a large cardboard model promoting a new line of low-carb, ready-to-drink shakes and supplements. On any other day, she might be tempted to add a box or two to the basket she'd grabbed on the way in, but in light of what she'd just seen in aisle three, calorie counting was the last thing on her mind.

Max pulled his arm away from her grip. "What is it?"

"Up ahead." She jutted her chin toward the next aisle.

"Why are we hiding? It's just Michelle—"

"Shh." She peeked around the cardboard model's bulky bicep before grabbing Max's arm again and pulling him next to her. "She's not alone."

Michelle stood beside a row of cold medicine, talking in hushed tones to a man. Late thirties, graying goatee, five-foot-seven at the most. It was the way Michelle stood that made Pricilla assume that this conversation was more than just an encounter with a friend at the store. She tried to make out what they were saying but couldn't follow the garbled whispers.

"Maybe it's a boyfriend," Max said.

Pricilla shook her head. "Sarah told me this morning that Michelle has a fiancé, but he's not supposed to be in town. We've got to get closer so we can hear what they are saying."

"Pricilla—"

She ignored his warning and slid past the bronze hunk until she was partly masked behind a shelf of diet pills. She paused to listen. Still too far away.

"Pricilla."

She swung her elbow around sharply to jab him to be quiet. Too sharply. She gasped. A display of diet drinks tumbled from the shelf, smacking the floor loudly before scattering in every direction.

Michelle's chin jerked up. One can rolled across the shiny surface and stopped at Pricilla's feet. She searched for the source of the commotion. Pricilla wanted to hide, but it was too late. Mr. Muscle tipped over, leaving her—and Max—exposed.

And looking completely guilty.

Another drink teetered on the shelf before plunging to the floor. It burst open against the tile floor and splattered as it rolled across the aisle, spraying chocolate across the bottom of Pricilla's skirt.

Great.

"Mrs. Crumb?"

"Michelle. You. . .you startled me."

"I startled *you*?" Michelle glanced up at her companion and then back to Pricilla as if she wasn't sure what to make of the situation.

"Cleanup in aisle three," boomed over the loud speaker. Pricilla spotted a back door that presumably led outside and wondered if anyone would notice if she sneaked out of the store. Probably. She glanced behind her. Where was Max?

She might as well take advantage of the situation. "I haven't met your friend."

"My friend. . ." Michelle glanced at the man. "No. . . he's not. . .we both just happened to be buying. . .cold medicine. I asked him which brand he recommended."

"Yes. Cold medicine." The man sneezed before grabbing a box of cold medicine and striding away toward the cashier.

"Cold medicine?" Pricilla repeated.

Michelle coughed. "Some brands will actually prevent a cold if you catch it early enough. I can't get sick right now, you know."

Pricilla frowned. The woman was lying.

"You're not sick, are you?" Michelle asked.

Changing the subject?

"Sick. . .no. Of course, not. I'm here with Max. He needed some antacids." Pricilla forced a smile as she stepped out of the way of the young clerk who'd been assigned to clean up the aisle and mumbled her apologies. "You know how it is with all the rich foods we've been sampling."

"I wouldn't know, actually. I've been having the kitchen prepare my own low-fat meals."

Pricilla nodded, not surprised at all with the confession.

"We start again in just over an hour," Michelle reminded her.

"And I'll be ready."

"Good. I don't think I can handle any more surprises."

Pricilla didn't want to handle any more surprises either, but neither was she quite ready to end the conversation. "I can't imagine how difficult the past two days have been for you, as the director of the competition, in losing both a judge and one of the contestants."

A hint of fatigue showed beneath Michelle's eyes. "Out of all the things I imagined going wrong, murder never once popped into the picture."

"I don't suppose it would." Pricilla swallowed. It was time to push for answers. "I understand, though, that you had a fight with Norton the night of the murder."

Michelle's face paled. "That sounds like another accusation, Mrs. Crumb."

"Not at all." Pricilla prayed she hadn't just pushed the woman too far. "I just thought it interesting that you had a fight with the victim the night he was killed and never told the sheriff."

"Not that's it's any of your business, but Norton and I were fighting over the show's credits. He believed his name should be highlighted on the rolling credits at the end."

"What did you do after the fight?"

"That's none of your business, Mrs. Crumb. But Norton and I fighting isn't exactly headline news. Anyone who knows me also knows that Norton and I never got along."

"Never?"

Michelle's knuckles whitened as she grasped her shopping basket tighter. "What are you implying now?"

"I understood that at one time you and Norton were. . . how shall I put it. . .more than friends."

Michelle took a step back. "I've done what I had to do to get where I am. Hiring him for this job was no different. I knew he'd boost the ratings."

"Which might have worked if he hadn't been murdered."

"It did work." Michelle smiled for the first time. "In an odd sort of way, hiring him became the one bright side of all this mess."

Max appeared beside Pricilla with a box of antacids. "The bright side of what?"

"With the murder of Norton Richards, the show's received more publicity than I ever imagined." Michelle's smile spread into a wide smirk. "It's a bit of poetic justice in a way, if you ask me."

"Meaning?" Pricilla asked.

"That something good actually came from Norton's death."

Pricilla frowned. "Well, I for one have a hard time imagining murder ever having a bright side."

"Ratings are up by twenty-five percent."

"Well. . .that's good." Or so she thought. It was a bit difficult to care about ratings with a man dead and Clarissa sitting in jail.

"One hour, Mrs. Crumb. And don't be late."

Pricilla glanced at Michelle's basket as she walked

away—without a box of cold medicine. "That was strange. She was actually happy, in a weird sort of way."

"So what do you think?" Max asked. "That Michelle killed Norton in order to boost ratings?"

"Weirder things have happened."

*Still. . .*Pricilla frowned. *Surely Michelle wouldn't have sabotaged the show by getting rid of Norton no matter how mad the man made her. Or would she?* Despite Michelle's innocent stance, the murder had brought the competition into the spotlight. Perhaps that had been her plan all the time. Killing two birds with one stone.

Pricilla fastened her seat belt before leaning back against the seat and closing her eyes. The sun filtering through the window felt warm against her face but did little to ease the chill of reality that swept over her from the constant reminders of Norton's untimely death. Her lip twitched. For a moment, she was there again. Clarissa stood over Norton's body. Red blood. A scream. . .

She popped open her eyes. Closing them only brought back the scene. Something she didn't want to experience again. Instead, she stared out the window at the passing aspen trees, dwarfed by the majestic mountains behind them, and forced her mind to think in another direction. But no matter how hard she tried, the normally vibrant spring mountainside blurred into muted colors and took her in directions she didn't want to go. She glanced over at Max, who clenched the steering wheel hard enough to make his knuckles turn white. Chin set, jaw taut, gaze pointed straight ahead. She knew the situation had him on edge. He wasn't the only one. What if she'd gotten everything wrong? What if Clarissa had actually killed Norton?

No. No matter what the DA thought, she refused to believe Clarissa was guilty. Call it gut instinct, or simple intuition, but she hadn't lived sixty-five years without picking up a thing or two about human nature. She knew she was right. The police might have a monopoly on forensics and lab reports, and she'd be the first to admit that their scientific tactics made sense, but there were times when a routine investigation missed the subtle interactions, background, and volatile relationships of a suspect. And that was where she came into the picture.

Certain she was headed in the right direction, Pricilla shifted her thoughts to Michelle. "You know that woman was lying."

The car's tires grated against the gravel as Max turned onto the road leading toward the lodge. "Who's lying? Michelle?"

Pricilla nodded.

Max shrugged. "Maybe the guy was a boyfriend, and for whatever reason, she didn't want anyone to know. It makes sense. The press has taken an interest in her and the show, and while she seems to enjoy the publicity, I can understand her wanting to keep her personal life out of the limelight."

"So they arrange a secret rendezvous in the cold-remedy section of the local pharmacy?" She definitely wasn't buying that line of thinking. From what she knew about Michelle, the woman would take publicity in any shape or form. "Doesn't seem likely. Besides, apparently Michelle is engaged to some guy named Charlie. Sarah said that he called this morning to tell her that he wasn't going to be able to make it. He's playing some gig down south."

Max's brows rose. "A gig?"

"Apparently he's a musician."

"I know what a gig is. I just can't see Michelle, of all people, married to a drummer, or some electric guitar player. But either way, isn't there a possibility that Charlie changed his mind and decided to come?"

"I suppose." While Pricilla wasn't ready to entirely

dismiss the boyfriend angle, that didn't seem likely.

"There's also another alternative."

"What's that?"

"Maybe the man was really who she said he was. Someone she ran into and asked advice on which was the better cold medicine."

Pricilla sighed. Of course he was probably right. All she'd managed to do was turn a typical encounter with a stranger into some top-secret meeting between two murder suspects.

"And you know that makes more sense than your clandestine meeting. If you start looking for trouble in every direction, then all you'll be doing is throwing another log onto an already out-of-control bonfire. Who that man was really isn't any of our business."

"You would be right except for the fact that we are in the middle of a murder investigation, and Michelle has already lied about her past relationship with Norton. I still think she has something to hide."

The gate to the lodge came into view, and Max slowed down. "I have to admit that I agree with you on that account, but your responsibility is simply to tell the sheriff what you saw and let him take it from there. That was the deal, remember?"

"Max—"

"No. All you are to do is pass on information. Sheriff Lewis is perfectly capable of doing the rest."

"I suppose." How many times was she going to have to back down and admit that he was right? Hadn't she gotten herself into enough trouble the past few days? Still, there was one thing she wouldn't forget. Clarissa was innocent, which meant there was still a murderer on the loose.

Five minutes later, Pricilla left Max in the lobby of the lodge and took the elevator to the second floor, wishing she didn't have yet another contest to emcee tonight. While she'd looked forward to the opportunity for months, Norton's death had managed to strip all the excitement from the event. And seeing Clarissa in jail had put an additional negative spin on things as well. She was now more determined than ever to ensure the young woman was found innocent, but with a growing pool of suspects, the truth seemed more and more evasive.

Pricilla stepped out of the elevator and stopped. Sarah stood in front of her, her arms loaded with books, files, and an expensive-looking silver cashmere sweater.

For the first time since she'd met the young girl Friday, Sarah's perky smile appeared forced. "So we meet again, Mrs. Crumb."

Pricilla shot her a sympathetic gaze. The young woman's work, it seemed, never ended. "I am sensing a bit of déjà vu."

Sarah's laugh rang as flat as her smile. "Michelle just called. We still have just under an hour until the next competition, but she's already got me rushing around."

"Maybe she's running behind. I saw her a few minutes ago in town." Pricilla decided to test the waters. "I thought you told me that Michelle's fiancé wasn't coming."

Sarah's eyes widened. "He's not."

"So he didn't change his mind and decide to show up?"

Sarah managed to reposition her glasses on the bridge of her nose with a swipe of her hand. "Far as I know, he's still in Texas. Trust me, if Charlie was coming I'd know. That six-foot-four cowboy doesn't make an entrance without a certain amount of fanfare, even if most of it is a figment of his own imagination."

"Six-foot-four cowboy?" That answered that question. Whoever Michelle had been with definitely wasn't Charlie.

Sarah shifted the load in her arms and eyed the elevator that had just closed. "Is there a problem?"

"No, of course not."

Pricilla pushed the button to open the door for Sarah, wondering how much information she should disclose. Considering the young woman was in the midst of negotiating an unauthorized biography about Norton, Sarah might be a great source of information, but Pricilla refused to be another conduit for gossip.

"It's nothing, really." Pricilla decided to drop the subject for now. "I'm sure she just must be disappointed."

The doors slid open and Sarah stepped into the doorway. "Trust me. Michelle can handle disappointment. Her skin's as tough as an alligator's."

Or so she wanted everyone to think.

Pricilla gnawed on her lip as the doors shut again, wondering what her next move should be. A glance down at her skirt gave her the answer she was looking for. She hadn't planned to change, but after her encounter with the milkshake mix on aisle three, it was necessary. Not that it really mattered. She was in the mood for something more subdued than the colorful silk blouse and deep purple skirt and jacket. Pulling the key card from her bag, she drew in a deep breath. She needed to put Michelle out of her mind for now, change her clothes, freshen up, and finish the day's last contest. Surely she could do that, though she had no idea how she was going to focus on her role as emcee when there was a murder to solve.

Pricilla shoved open the door. Trisha stood in the middle of the room dressed in her wedding dress with its ripples of glossy fabric around the floor while Riley made adjustments on a sleeve.

"Mrs. Crumb. It's good to see you again." Riley pulled a straight pin from her mouth and smiled.

"It's nice to see you, Riley, as well. It looks as if you're almost done with the gown."

"It's beautiful, isn't it?" Trisha's smile widened.

"One more fitting and I think we'll be finished. Trisha and I decided to change the drape a bit, and I wanted to make sure everything still fit correctly. We don't want any last-minute surprises, you know."

"You're right about that." Pricilla chuckled and set her bag down on the desk.

She crossed the room toward her closet, unable to keep her eyes off the gown. She stopped midway on the thick carpet. "It really is stunning, Riley. Absolutely stunning."

Trisha's dreamy smile spoke volumes. "I told Riley I was going to feel like a genuine princess on my wedding day because of her."

"Which is exactly how you should feel. Young, beautiful, and glamorous."

Pricilla laughed. "I'm glad someone in the room feels both young and beautiful at the same time. Enjoy it."

Riley took a step back and hit the bedside table, knocking her pair of shears to the floor.

Pricilla reached to pick them up and then ran her hand across the material. It was time she found something to wear at her own wedding. Up until now, she'd focused all her energy on her job at the lodge and helping Trisha with the unending details of her and Nathan's wedding. Maybe she could find time for a day trip into Denver during the next couple of weeks. While Trisha's gown was far too elaborate for what Pricilla wanted, there was no reason she couldn't find something simple, yet at the same time, beautiful.

Riley took a step back from Trisha's slender form. "Do you like it, Mrs. Crumb?"

"Do I like it? It's exquisite. I was just thinking about my own wedding and how I need to start looking for my own dress in the next few weeks."

"There's no reason why you can't have something just as beautiful." Riley made another small tuck before slipping a straight pin into the top of the sleeve. "If you ask me, beauty is timeless."

"Maybe Riley could design something for you, Mom."

Pricilla smiled at the term of endearment Trisha had begun calling her. "At sixty-five, I don't think I need something quite this. . .fancy, but it is time I found a dress."

In fact, there were still dozens of details left to be worked out—and just a month before the wedding! She felt a rush of adrenaline. She might be sixty-five, but that was no reason for her not to look forward to her own upcoming nuptials.

Riley set down her pin cushion. "I'd offer to make you a dress, but starting next week I have an entire wedding party to outfit. I'm going to have my hands full for the next few weeks."

Thoughts of eloping flittered through Pricilla's mind once again. Maybe it wasn't such a bad idea. A trip to the notary public might sound a bit unromantic, but the bottom line was that a marriage was far more important than the actual wedding ceremony. What she was looking forward to was the companionship that came with marriage. Marty had been that for so many years, and it was something she missed. Max had managed to not only fill that need, but the emptiness in her heart, as well.

Pricilla pulled a cinnamon brown pantsuit from the closet and headed for the bathroom. "If the two of you will excuse me, I need to change for my last spot as emcee for the night."

"Is it going all right?" Riley turned from the dress and caught Pricilla's gaze. "What I mean is, with a murder taking place right here. . .well. . .it has to change the dynamics of the event, even if the murderer is behind bars."

"That's the problem, he's not!"

"He's not?"

"The murderer. He. . .she. . .I don't know who it is at this point, but it's not Clarissa."

Riley's eyes widened. "You sound certain."

"I am."

"That's exactly what we've been discussing." Trisha ran her painted fingernails along the bodice of her dress. "I told Riley about our excursion in the lake and the knife."

"Any other new developments?" Riley asked.

"No. Not really." Pricilla sat down on the edge of the bed, her plans to change clothes momentarily postponed. She wasn't ready to mention her suspicions about Michelle, at least not to anyone other than the sheriff. More than likely, Max was right, and she was following a dead end. "I'm just worried about Clarissa. I visited her in jail today and the poor girl is at her wit's end."

"I can't imagine what she's going through," Trisha said. "Especially if she's innocent. Can you imagine being accused of something you didn't do, then end up having to go to jail because of it?"

Pricilla shuddered. No, she couldn't. The closest she'd ever come to the inside of a prison cell was when she'd borrowed—or rather, stolen—an ATV from the rental shop in Rendezvous. At the moment, the impulsive act had seemed necessary. Looking back, she knew there had to have been a better way to deal with the situation, which was a viewpoint that both Detective Carter and Max had made very clear to her.

Pricilla got up and hurried down to the lobby in better spirits. With Trisha's wedding taken care of, it was time to concentrate on herself and Max. Something she planned to do just as soon as this contest was over.

The sheriff caught her on her way down the hall. "Mrs. Crumb. I was just on my way out. Do you have a minute?"

Pricilla glanced at her watch. "I'm not due in front of the camera for another twenty minutes, but I can't be late this time. I'm hoping that our finding the knife in the lake will help Clarissa's case, but Michelle wasn't impressed with my appearance after I fell into the lake."

"I'm sorry about that." The lawman fiddled with the brim of his hat between his hands. "But I still owe you a tremendous thanks for what you did."

"Do you think the knife will help Clarissa's case?"

"I hope so."

"You hope so?" Pricilla fought back the frustration. While she understood that there could be no guarantees at this point, she'd thought the evidence would tip things more in Clarissa's favor. "You don't sound very positive."

"We're certain now that the knife you found came from Clarissa's kitchen."

"Which doesn't prove she killed Norton."

"No. And you're right in that it should help her case. If the knife had been found closer to the crime scene, things would probably be more cut-and-dried. As it is, the DA realizes that there was no way for Clarissa to kill Norton and dispose of the knife so far away."

As much as she didn't want to, Pricilla had to ask another question. "What about the possibility that she killed him, disposed of the knife, and then returned to make it look like she didn't do it?"

"The coroner believes there wouldn't have been time for her to kill him, throw the knife in the lake, and return to the point where you saw her standing over him."

"Then that should be our proof. Right?"

"Or, according to the DA, it implies that someone else was involved. Her lawyer is doing everything he can to get her released because of lack of evidence, but in the end we may be looking at a trial." The sheriff's expression tightened. "Any news for me?"

"There are a couple of things I'm worried about." A small group Pricilla had noticed from the contest's audience entered the lobby, making a lot of noise. Pricilla followed the sheriff down the empty, long hallway toward the Great Room to ensure they were out of earshot from anyone. "There have been more instances where I believe Michelle has been lying."

"You've got my attention."

Pricilla shared with the sheriff her concerns about Michelle.

The sheriff paused halfway down the hallway and shoved his hands into his front pockets. "It's not a crime to lie about who you're talking to, but in the case of her not disclosing her relationship to Norton, I am concerned. Maybe it's nothing more than her being embarrassed, but in a murder investigation, that's no excuse for lying."

"I definitely agree."

Withholding evidence and lying to the authorities were things Michelle would know were serious offenses. Had her lies sprouted from a guilty conscience? Or had they surfaced because of fear that her relationship with Norton would be seen as a motive to kill him?

"How did you find Clarissa?"

Pricilla noted the genuine concern in the man's voice as they started walking again. At least he seemed to believe in Clarissa's innocence. "Understandably, this has not been easy for her. She's a small-town girl way out of her league. I'm worried about her."

"So am I."

This time Pricilla heard a catch in the sheriff's voice. Something wasn't right. This wasn't simply another case for the sheriff.

"What is it? Is this case personal for you?"

The sheriff glanced behind him and then stopped again. "I'm not sure. . . ."

"What is it?"

"You're right that this case has become too personal. I've asked a colleague of mine to take it over for me."

"Why? Clarissa needs someone who believes in her."

"I know. The fact is, though, there's a problem with my working the case. Clarissa. . . I should have volunteered to step aside immediately, but I couldn't have Clarissa found guilty for something I know she didn't do." The sheriff combed his fingers through his hair. "Clarissa is my daughter from my first marriage."

12

The sheriff's confession caught Pricilla completely off guard. On the other hand, the man had seemed overly anxious to ensure that Clarissa wasn't convicted for Norton's murder. Now she knew why.

The sheriff's gaze darted to the floor in what she interpreted as a moment of regret over the admission. Or perhaps his guilty expression had more to do with regrets over the past. She pressed her lips together, determined to give him a moment to compose his thoughts while at the same time wishing she could remember what Clarissa's mother had told her about her first husband. Back then, she'd never expected to meet the man, let alone work with him, even if it was only in an unofficial capacity. Which was probably exactly why he'd been willing for her to help in the first place.

The sheriff cleared his throat and slowly raised his head until he caught her gaze. Pain, guilt, and remorse mingled in his eyes. "Clarissa was five months old when her mother and I divorced. It was. . .and still is. . .a moment I've spent my entire life regretting."

Pricilla glanced down the hallway to make certain no one was in earshot of their conversation. The staff was already preparing for the next competition in the Great Room, but their attention wasn't focused on the decades-old confessions of Sheriff Lewis. "Do you want to tell me what happened?"

He leaned against the wall, drew in a deep breath, and then let it out slowly. "Judy and I had been married three months when she found out we were expecting. We'd wanted kids, but not for several years. At the time, I didn't know if I should be angry, or happy. . .or what."

"It must have been a very stressful time for both of you."

"Yeah. You could say that."

His tanned brow furrowed as he motioned toward a set of glass doors and beyond, to a bench surrounded by rows of lush plants. Pricilla glanced at her watch. Clarissa was certainly a priority over the current food competition, but that didn't erase her concern of not fulfilling her commitment to Michelle. Thankfully, she still had a few minutes before the next contest.

He opened the door, and they stepped out into the breezy afternoon air. The sun sparkled against the water that lay below the majestic Rocky Mountains, but for now, she was more interested in what Sheriff Lewis had to say than the stunning view. A counseling session with law enforcement was the last thing she'd expected today.

He rotated his hat in his hand and sat down beside her on the bench. "I was trying to get into the police academy; she was working as a secretary. At first, even with the unexpected pregnancy, it didn't seem to matter that we were poor and living on macaroni and cheese. What's the old saying? Love covers a multitude of *sins*?"

Pricilla frowned at the emphasized word. "Sins?"

He glanced up at her. "Unfortunately, it's not always true."

"What do you mean?"

The sheriff stared at a group of lean aspen trees. "I've always said that the discipline of four years in the military and a career in law enforcement have been my salvation, but before that, I grew up with a bit of a temper and didn't have it under control when I married Judy. Losing her wasn't the first time my impulsiveness got me into trouble."

Pricilla winced. The confession struck too close to home. She'd fought her own battles with impulsiveness and almost lost Max in the process. What was it about human nature that made one tend to choose the wayward path?

His blue eyes seemed to pierce right through her. "Have you ever accused someone of doing something they didn't do?"

She hesitated at the question. "I don't know. I'm sure I have."

"I started drinking from stress, until one afternoon I lost my temper and accused Judy of seeing someone else. That the baby wasn't mine." The following pause was full of emotion. "I'd been jealous of her boss's attention, and while it had bordered on inappropriate, I never asked for her side of the story. Things got out of hand during that discussion and accusations flared. The bottom line was that I hadn't trusted her. She never forgave me for that."

"I'm so sorry."

"So am I. My impulsiveness lost me my wife and my daughter. In the end, we divorced, and I moved here."

"Did you ever see Clarissa again?"

The sheriff shook his head. "Judy remarried a year later. I decided that it would be better for all of us if I just walked out of their lives for good. I didn't want to compete with a stepfather. Now I wish I'd stayed around and been a part of her life."

"What about you? Did you ever remarry?"

"I finally got my act together through a local AA

program and a preacher who wouldn't leave me alone. I met Paula at a singles' meeting at church shortly after I became a Christian. We have two boys, Seth and Michael, who are fourteen and sixteen."

Pricilla smiled. "That's wonderful, though I can't imagine how tough it must have been for you."

"At least Clarissa was too young to understand what was going on when I walked out. The bottom line is that Bruce is her father. She doesn't know about me."

"Doesn't seem fair somehow."

"In my years of law enforcement, I learned not only to curb my temper, but that life is rarely fair." Sheriff Lewis cleared his throat before standing. "Mrs. Crumb, look. I'm sorry for all of this."

"Sorry?"

"I shouldn't be dumping my problems on you. It's just that seeing Clarissa was such a shock. Especially when I was the one forced to arrest her. And seeing her again, well, it managed to drag me back to a past I thought I'd put behind me." He shook his head. "I have no right to drag you into my personal life."

"Please." Pricilla waved her hand in dismissal as she stood to join him. "What's important right now is that we do everything we can to help Clarissa, which I know is exactly what you want. Can I ask you a question?"

"Of course."

"How did you know she was your daughter?"

"I've been in touch with Judy off and on throughout the years. She sent me a photo of her two years ago. Clarissa had just graduated and had a job as a sous-chef. Judy thought I'd like to see how well Clarissa turned out despite the mistakes I made."

"Mistakes you both made," Pricilla underscored. "Are you going to let her know?"

"That I'm her father?" His eyes widened.

"Yes."

"I don't know—"

"I think you should."

"She's already gone through so much. . . ."

"Maybe. But what I do know is she needs people who believe in her." The five-minute warning bell rang. "I have to leave. Michelle will never forgive me for missing another session."

"Of course."

"I want Clarissa freed as much as you. She didn't do it."

"I don't know her the way you do, but I know you're right." He pressed his hat down onto his head. "And we have to find out the truth. Quickly."

⟡

Max strained his neck to see over the stocky man sitting in front of him who no doubt was enjoying the weekend with its large choice of gourmet samples. At the moment, though, Max's mind was far from appetizers and succulent entrees. Pricilla was—once again—missing. The past two days had proved to him that she'd still failed to put a curb on her impulsive tendencies. That had been emphasized by the fire alarm escapade and finding the murder weapon in the lake. Did he really want to live with that? He glanced past the man again. The five-minute warning bell had gone off at least four minutes ago, and she was still not in her place at the microphone.

He was rising to leave when he saw someone hurry

across the left of the stage. The following flood of relief that swept over him managed to extinguish any anger that had briefly made him wonder if his heart would be able to handle life with Pricilla.

Her smile reached him and he melted. The past few days had wound his nerves into knots. Between murder victims, butcher knives, and her exploits, the weekend was far from what he'd envisioned when he agreed to a relaxing minivacation in the mountains. At least he wouldn't have to call on the cavalry this time to search for her. But in spite of the fact she was there in front of him, he was still worried. More than likely he was the only one who could tell that her warm expression was slightly forced. He returned her smile, hoping it would give her the boost of energy she needed. The bottom line was that Pricilla would always be Pricilla, and he wouldn't want it any other way.

She looked every bit the professional she'd been when he first met her almost forty years ago. Back then she'd organized yearly baking competitions for her girls at the academy but probably never expected that she'd one day be standing in front of a television audience. No one would guess this was her first time to do so.

Pricilla addressed the audience with the same poise and grace Max had admired all those years ago. "Ladies and gentlemen, welcome again to the Fifteenth Annual Rocky Mountain Chef Competition. This next competition is one of my favorites, and as I've observed in years past, I'm sure it is many of yours as well. It's the contestants who are sweating under their white coats."

The audience laughed on cue.

"Now we all know they can cook." Pricilla moved to

the side of the podium, seeming to enjoy the interaction from the audience. "The question is, can they handle the pressure of cooking both an appetizer and a main course with only the ingredients found in these black boxes." A couple of audible gasps erupted from the audience as she continued. "So welcome to this afternoon's Black-box Competition, where it's all about improvising, nerves of steel, and of course, creating a winning dish.

"Every contestant must utilize all the ingredients in the box and will have exactly two hours to prepare a feast that will be served to both our judges and those holding tickets to tonight's gala. Points will then be awarded by the judges for taste, skill, creativity, and finally, artistic merit. And now for the list of ingredients. . .Michelle, the envelope please."

The audience hushed as Michelle handed a black envelope to Pricilla. The contestants stood before their boxes, the tension obvious on their faces. With a quarter of a million dollars at stake, it was no wonder. Pricilla slit open the envelope, pausing briefly to raise the anticipation before reading. "Here are the long-awaited ingredients of this year's Black-box Competition. Pork loin, smoked salmon, fresh prawns, calamari, asparagus, shallots, baby beets, onions, red potatoes, mushrooms, pear, mango, yellow—"

A loud *pop* exploded throughout the room. Max jumped from his chair. Someone screamed. It only took him a few seconds to realize the source of the commotion. Christopher Jeffries's stove was engulfed in flames.

Twenty minutes later, Max was sitting in on a meeting between the sheriff, Michelle, the hotel manager, and Pricilla. He reached for his fourth cup of coffee of the day. At this rate, he was going to be jittery from all the caffeine, but for the moment he needed something to do with his hands. The whole experience had him completely unnerved.

"How could this have happened?" Michelle paced the narrow meeting room.

Pricilla pulled out the cushioned chair beside her and motioned to Michelle. "Why don't you sit down? All you're going to do at this point is end up with a bill for the hole in the carpet."

Michelle grasped the back of the chair. "You all don't understand."

Max cleared his throat before injecting his opinion. "From what I've seen, the publicity of the show is anything but suffering."

"That might be true, but this has turned into a circus, which was not what I had in mind, publicity or not."

The sheriff held up his hand. "There's no use arguing. What we do need to do is to find out the truth about what is going on here."

"The situation is perfectly clear to me." Michelle finally plopped down on the offered chair.

"What are you talking about?" the sheriff asked.

"Someone's trying to sabotage my show."

"That has yet to be proven, but why would someone do that?"

She leaned forward and shot the lawman a heated glare. "If we knew why, none of us would be sitting here right now, would we?"

The sheriff frowned, grabbing his notebook. "Even I will admit that you might be on track about sabotage, a scheme that just might be working. I know I'm tempted to close down the competition."

Michelle shot up from her chair. "There is no way I will allow you to put a stop to my competition. I've worked too hard for this to be thrown down the tubes because of a few problems."

"A few problems?" The sheriff's brow furrowed. "Might I remind you, Miss Vanderbilt, that not only was one of your judges murdered, we just had an explosion that could have sent a man to the hospital. It's a miracle he wasn't hurt more than a few singed hairs."

"Believe me, I know. I almost lost another contestant."

Max frowned at the woman's coldness. A man could have been killed, and all she cared about was his worth as a contestant.

Pricilla leaned back in her chair. "Is it possible that Norton's death isn't related to the mishaps in the kitchen?"

The sheriff flipped through his notebook as if searching for an elusive answer to the problem. "I've considered the possibility. But there is also the possibility that these two latest incidents were nothing but accidents."

Michelle stood over him. "Do you really believe that, sheriff? Because I for one am convinced that someone is out to sabotage my show, and I want to know what you are going to do to ensure I can finish my contest without any more incidents. Because if you can't—"

"Miss Vanderbilt, sit down." The sheriff combed his fingers through his hair. "Please."

Michelle hesitated and then complied without another word.

"Thank you. I'm already ahead of you. I'm posting a guard outside the kitchen for starters. No one will be allowed to enter the competition area without their official badge."

"That's a good first step."

"And there's one other thing. The other reason I called you all in here was to let you know that Michael Tanner, a good friend and colleague of mine who works for the local police, will be taking over the case as soon as I can brief him."

Max glanced at Pricilla, who didn't look surprised at all. Michelle, on the other hand, looked livid. "Don't tell me you're quitting the investigation."

"For personal reasons I won't go into. . .yes, I am. We'll leave it at that for now. I'll make sure Tanner knows everything that's gone on here, and in return, I expect full cooperation—and truthfulness—to be given to him."

Michelle squirmed in her seat and then turned away, avoiding the sheriff's telling gaze and leaving Max to wonder what else the woman was hiding.

Sleepless nights had become all too common. Pricilla glanced at the red glow of the clock beside the bed and groaned. Despite her concern over the turmoil of the day, she'd finally managed to fall asleep, but now, two hours later, she was wide awake again.

Pulling on her tennis shoes and a comfy track suit, she took the elevator down to the lobby to see if it was possible to get some hot milk to help her sleep. She passed the lodge's gym on the way, noticed the light was on, and wondered how anyone could be working out at this hour. She looked through the window and saw Maggie

Underwood running on the treadmill.

Pricilla poked her head inside the room that contained a couple of treadmills, a stationary bike, and a few weight machines. "I see I'm not the only one who can't sleep."

Maggie's smile was bright despite the late hour. "Exercise has always been relaxing to me. Seemed like the best thing to do to combat my nerves."

"I don't blame you. It's been a tough couple of days." Pricilla leaned back against the treadmill next to Maggie. "You ended up doing well early today. I loved your prawn and calamari soup."

"Thanks, but even that dish probably won't be enough to win the competition. I'm afraid I'm too far behind at this point." Maggie punched a button and her speed increased to a jog. "It's hard to believe I could lose $250,000 over a pan of burned raspberry sauce." Maggie glanced at the other treadmill. "Why don't you jump on for a few minutes? Then I won't feel as if I'm the only crazy person working out when it's past midnight."

"Exercise...I..." Pricilla glanced at the updated version of a treadmill she once had. Hers had turned out to be the perfect coatrack in the winter. "This machine is awfully... high tech. I'm used to walking outside."

Maggie leaned over and punched a button on the machine. The screen lit up. Pricilla took a step backward.

"They might seem a bit complicated at first, but don't let that scare you off," Maggie said. "My grandmother still walks five miles a day on hers while watching soap operas."

"Really...?"

"Here you go. All you have to do is step on and push this button." Maggie nodded as she reached for her water bottle.

"I don't know—"

"Start off slow. You'll get the hang of it before you know it."

Pricilla hesitated before stepping onto the machine. She'd given up going to the gym ages ago, settling instead for frequent walks along the wooded paths near Nathan's lodge. Maybe this wouldn't be any different. There were several more things she wanted to ask the young woman, and at the moment, a midnight jaunt on the treadmill was looking like her only option. Even if her muscles still ached from the fall into the lake.

"You're sure it will start off slow?"

"Positive."

Pricilla stepped onto the machine, hesitated another two seconds, and then pushed the START button. This was great. It was twelve thirty at night, and she had to walk—or land in a heap at the other end of the machine. But it did start off slowly like Maggie had said. Maybe this wouldn't be so bad after all.

Pricilla worked to catch her breath and forced in a lungful of air. Maggie hadn't missed a step. Oh, to be thirty-something again with no cellulite, clog-free arteries, and a pulse like an athlete. For now she'd have to settle for a few extra pounds around the waist, crow's-feet, and blood pressure that tended to rise in stressful situations. Like a weekend filled with murder and mayhem.

"Did you know Norton?" Pricilla finally managed to ask.

"I met him once, though I know he'd never remember me."

"Why's that?"

"He held a public signing for the book he published a couple years ago. I'd always liked his reviews. Brutal, yes, but honest. And definitely interesting. I always wanted to be a chef and figured I could learn from the man. Besides that, I suppose it's always been every chef's secret fantasy to get a rave review from Norton."

"I'm beginning to see that." Her breathing was becoming shallower. So much for her power walks through the mountains. "Any takes on his murderer?"

Maggie upped the speed on her treadmill. She must be kin to Wonder Woman. "You really don't think Clarissa did it?"

"No, I don't."

"I don't have a take on the murderer, but I do have another, shall we say, *ethical situation* I'm facing."

Pricilla fought to focus on the conversation and not the moving belt beneath her. "What do you mean?"

"I. . .I haven't told anyone this yet, because it just happened. That's why I'm here, trying to decide if I'm overreacting or if Freddie is really up to something."

Pricilla looked down and tried to stop the ensuing panic. Her shoe was untied. She fumbled for the STOP button. Her speed increased. "Maggie! Get me off this thing. . . ."

"Mrs. Crumb—"

"Now. . .please. . ."

Maggie pushed STOP on her own machine and leaped off in one easy bound. A few seconds later, Pricilla's came to a stop. She glanced down at her shoe. At least she was still upright and in one piece. She had panicked, maybe, but at the moment, she didn't feel as if she could be too careful.

Maggie held on to her forearm. "Are you all right?"

"I'm fine. Computers, treadmills, and well, anything electronic—except for a good oven—let's just say that I've never really gotten along with any of them." She sat down on the weight bench and tried to catch her breath. "What were you saying about Freddie?"

Maggie grabbed her towel to wipe away the perspiration on her forehead. "I overheard him arguing with Lyle Simpson, one of the judges, about an hour ago."

Pricilla frowned. Everyone knew the strict rules forbidding any interaction between contestants and judges. "What were they arguing about?"

Maggie shrugged at the question. "I'm not sure exactly. Freddie said something about Lyle keeping his side of the bargain. There were a few more harsh words exchanged, but that was the gist of what I heard. What bothers me, of course, is that Freddie knows he'll be kicked out of the competition if Michelle finds out they were talking. We all even had to sign forms that we would have no contact with the judges under any circumstances."

"Including blackmail," Pricilla mumbled under her breath.

"Blackmail?"

"I'm sorry. I was just thinking out loud." Pricilla took the hand towel Maggie gave her and wiped off the back of her neck. "Don't worry about what you saw, Maggie. I'll take care of it."

"That would be great. I'd prefer not to be known as the snitch in the competition. Not that Freddie doesn't deserve to be put in his place. The man's insufferable."

Pricilla said good night before heading out of the gym and down the hall toward her room. Had Freddie been so intent on winning that he found a way to make an unscrupulous bargain that would guarantee it? If so,

Norton might have become the one thing standing in the way of winning.

A crash sounded on the other side of the lodge where the competition was held. Pricilla hesitated in front of the elevators. If Max were here he'd forbid her from investigating. But Max wasn't here.

A police officer rounded the corner, almost colliding with her. "Excuse me."

Pricilla pursed her lips. "Are you the officer on duty tonight?"

"Yes, I. . ." The man glanced back toward his post. "I just left to get a cup of coffee. . . ."

Pricilla rushed in front of the officer. "One cup of coffee might have just bought our murderer enough time to strike again."

13

The dimmed lights in the cathedral ceiling cast just enough of a yellow glow for Pricilla to make her way down the wide, carpeted hallway toward the kitchens. Max might disapprove of any late-night investigating, but at least this time she had reinforcements. The officer charged past her, his keys jingling at his side while he spat something into his radio, making more noise than a herd of elephants. So much for sneaking up on the suspect.

Something rattled, and this time it wasn't the set of keys. Someone was in the kitchens. A crash sounded again, like pots falling onto the tiled floor. Whoever it was must have bided his or her time until the officer left and then hurried to make a move. Ten more yards and they'd be there. But if they missed whoever had broken in. . .

Pricilla entered the room behind the officer and switched on the overhead flood lights, hoping to at least catch a glimpse of the perpetrator. She blinked, waiting for her eyes to adjust to the brightness.

The officer rushed into the kitchens that had been set up for the competition and shouted for the perpetrator to freeze. A door slammed shut. Whoever it was had just left the building.

Pricilla called for the officer to hurry.

"Don't worry, ma'am. I'll get 'em."

Pricilla started to follow but then stopped midstride. Her time on the treadmill had drained her of any energy she'd had left. She'd never be a match for a sprint across the lodge's grounds in the dark.

The officer returned a minute later shaking his head. "Whoever it was is gone. I wasn't even able to catch a glimpse of them."

Pricilla let out a sharp puff of air and then jumped as the sheriff's voice boomed behind her, "What's going on?"

She whirled around. "Sheriff Lewis. Don't you ever sleep?"

"Not lately." The shadows beneath his eyes were more pronounced than usual. Of course, hers probably were as well. "I suppose I could say the same for you. I was driving home and heard the message come in over Stew's radio."

Stew's gaze searched the ground. "They got away, Sheriff. I'm sorry."

"Man. . .woman. . .tall. . .short?"

Stew shook his head. "Nothing. I only caught a glimpse of a shadow."

"Well, that narrows it down." Displeasure shone in the sheriff's eyes as he turned to Pricilla. "And what about you, Mrs. Crumb? I told you I'd have one of my men working. What are you doing here?"

"I was on my way up to bed when I heard a crash." She glanced at the officer, not wanting to squeal on him, yet wondering if the sheriff needed to know that the man hadn't been at his post.

"And I was off getting a cup of coffee." The officer's confession saved her from saying anything.

"Coffee? We'll talk about that later." From the look the sheriff shot the officer, Pricilla was certain heads were going to roll before the night was over. "Did you see anything at all, Mrs. Crumb?"

"Just noises. Whoever it was must have heard us

coming and taken off." Pricilla cocked her head. "I thought you'd been taken off this case."

"I am. . .or shall I say I *was*. Sheriff Tanner was involved in a hit-and-run this afternoon. Broke both legs and will be off duty for the next few weeks."

"I'm sorry."

"So am I. Tanner's a good man. Until someone else is assigned, I'll be continuing with the case."

Which might give him time to prove Clarissa's innocence.

"You need to take a look at this, Sheriff." Stew had moved into the kitchen area.

"What is it?"

The three of them stepped over a pile of pans that had fallen to the floor. Whoever had broken in had left behind a blow torch.

Sheriff Lewis let out a low whistle. "It definitely looks as if someone was trying to sabotage one of the kitchens."

"You're right." Pricilla nodded. "Maggie's burned sauce. . .the explosion in Christopher's oven. . ."

"We can sweep the room for evidence, but I'm not sure we'll find anything that will help us. Dusting for prints won't tell us much either, as too many people have had access to this area."

"At least it gives us a direction to take the case."

"That's assuming that these incidents are even related to Richards's murder. But why would someone want to sabotage the contest? In order to shut things down?"

Pricilla yawned, but her mind was now wide awake. "Maybe there's another angle."

The sheriff quirked his left brow, obviously not

interested in having his night complicated any further.

"I found out an interesting tidbit tonight, though how it ties into this mess, I'm still not entirely certain."

The sheriff rubbed his eyes. The man was definitely overworked. The fact that his estranged daughter was in his jail had to exacerbate the fatigue. At least he was still on the case. Clarissa needed someone who would go the extra mile for her, and from everything Pricilla had seen so far, Sheriff Lewis was that person. "What is it?"

"Maggie overheard one of the judges, Lyle Simpson," Pricilla said. "He was talking to Freddie Longfellow about keeping his side of the bargain."

"What do you make of that?" the sheriff asked.

"Well for one, judges and contestants are strictly forbidden to interact at any point during the contest. Such behavior means immediate expulsion."

"Then why would they be talking?"

"That's what I want to know. The only thing I can think of is that they had some sort of unscrupulous deal going. Maybe a cut in the prize money."

"A huge presumption, but you might be on to something." The sheriff rubbed his chin. "If Lyle could somehow guarantee Freddie wins, then he'd take a cut of the prize money. But while it's not too hard to imagine $250,000 as motivation for breaking a few rules, how could one judge guarantee a win?"

Pricilla mulled over the question. "I don't know how they'd do it, but I suppose it might be possible. What I do know is for the whole competition, Freddie has had this cocky, I'm-going-to-win attitude."

"Which doesn't make him guilty but also doesn't dismiss the question, is he willing to do anything for the prize money?"

"Sabotaging the other contestants' workstations would give him the upper hand."

"So might murder. Especially if he believed, for whatever reason, that Norton might tip the votes the wrong way." He sighed. They both needed a good night's sleep, but after tonight, Pricilla feared that any rest would be hard to come by. "Whatever happened to good, old-fashioned bake-offs where the only prize was a blue ribbon for the best cherry pie in the county?"

"That's a good question," Pricilla said.

"For now, we all need to get to bed. Stew, don't leave your post. For anything. And call me if anything happens. I'll have your replacement here at five."

"Yes, sir."

"Tomorrow I'll bring Freddie and Lyle in separately for questioning to see if we can get somewhere with that angle. Does anything else look like it's been tampered with?"

Pricilla shook her head. "I don't think so, but it's hard to tell."

"I'm convinced whoever it was will be back."

"Then this time we better be ready."

⌐

Pricilla rounded the corner of the lobby the next morning and felt her breath catch. He stood at the edge of the room waiting for her. Coffee-colored Dockers, neatly pressed, buttoned-down shirt. . .and a wide smile just for her.

Her day suddenly brightened. "Morning, Max."

He handed her a cup of steaming coffee. "Morning to you, Bright Eyes."

Bright Eyes? She wished. She felt more like she'd just emerged from a dark tunnel and was ready to crawl back in.

Max's lingering kiss managed to give her an extra shot of energy, but not enough, she was afraid, to propel her through the rest of the day without a long afternoon nap. One she'd probably never get to take because of today's schedule. Max, on the other hand, looked ready to run a marathon.

She squeezed his hand. "You look chipper. Too chipper, in fact."

"Didn't you sleep well?" He took a sip of his coffee.

Pricilla stifled a yawn, hoping the caffeine helped. Where should she begin? With her late-night exercise jaunt at the gym with Maggie, the mishap in the kitchen when the perpetrator got away, or the hour and a half of trying to fall sleep while suspects and motives scurried through her mind, refusing to leave her alone?

She tried to fill him in briefly on all that had happened during the past eight hours.

A flicker of concern registered in Max's eyes. "Let's leave right now. We could head back to Nathan's lodge and spend the rest of the weekend doing nothing but fishing, hiking, and napping on the front porch. Michelle can take over for you here. She loves the spotlight and probably wouldn't mind at all. In fact, I'd go as far as to say that she'd jump at the chance."

For a moment, Pricilla let her mind linger on the idea. All she'd wanted was a quiet weekend with Max, walks around the lake, late-night talks, and conversation over some five-star food. . .definitely not murder. A wave of guilt replaced her wistful thinking. Her relaxing weekend might have been replaced with interviewing suspects and late-night excursions to hunt down suspects, but Clarissa sat in jail right now with the possibility of a decade or two of prison hanging over her.

Max would understand. He'd have to. She'd made a promise she was determined to keep.

"I wish I could leave with you, but you know I can't."

His smile forgave her. "I know. It seems to be my job to worry about you."

She chuckled. "What happened to the verse in the Bible that talks about not worrying about your life, or what you will eat—"

"I'm not worried about my life." He tipped her chin up with his thumb. "I'm worried about yours. Something I think God understands."

Blue eyes met hers. Her breath caught. "Then He also has to understand that I have to fulfill my commitment."

"I'm just concerned about you. Your proposed time to get away and relax has turned into chaos." He reached down and squeezed her hand. "And somehow I hadn't planned my retirement to be filled with sleuthing and undercover detective work."

"I know, Dr. Watson." She flashed him her best smile. "At least this is the last day of the competition."

The last day.

Reality hit hard. The four of them had made plans to attend church in Denver tomorrow where Nathan was friends with the pastor and then head back to Rendezvous after lunch. She could stay here and continue her investigation, but she had a commitment to Nathan as well. A large group was arriving at the lodge on Wednesday from back East, which didn't leave her much time to prepare. Misty, her assistant, would be there to help her, but she still had to shop for groceries, stop by the Baker's Dozen for bread and pastries, and start cooking for the dozen hungry appetites that were coming.

Which gave her today to find answers.

The five-minute warning bell rang.

"When's your next break?" Max asked.

She checked the schedule she'd carried downstairs. "The morning session lasts until ten thirty. Fondants, candy, and confectioners. Then all that's left is the afternoon's session and the award ceremony tonight."

"And tomorrow we can drive away from all of this."

Which brought her back again to the realization that she had far too little time to get to the bottom of who killed Norton Richards.

She gripped the schedule between her fingers. "What about Clarissa?"

"Her parents get in tonight. She'll be all right."

"But I promised her I'd help, Max—"

"You've risked your life helping her. You've done all you can. It's time to let the police do the rest."

Pricilla let out a soft "humph." She knew he was right, but that didn't erase the urgency she felt to find answers. She glanced up. Michelle scurried around in a peach suit, barking orders. At least she still had today.

Max watched the flutter of activity from the back row of the audience, thankful he had nothing to do with running the show. Michelle looked frazzled with only two minutes left before the cameras rolled. At least Pricilla was here. Despite her lack of sleep the night before, she still looked beautiful to him in her black checkered suit. The contestants, outfitted in their matching chef coats, black pants, and tall chef hats, were busy setting up their kitchens.

All except Freddie.

Max frowned as he leaned forward and scanned the kitchens again for a sign of the cocky chef. No. He'd been right. All the chefs were accounted for except for Freddie, who apparently was late. . .or missing. Max squeezed his eyes shut for a moment to erase the thought. Freddie wasn't missing. That assumption was coming from an imagination sparked by a weekend that had been anything but normal.

Michelle swore, catching his attention. Apparently she'd just noticed Freddie's absence as well. Forget that the entire audience could hear her every word or that they were about to go live in another—he checked his watch—one and a half minutes.

"He knows the rules," she snapped at the cameraman. "We'll start without him. Pricilla, you're on in one minute."

The sheriff slid into the seat beside Max. "What's wrong now?"

"Freddie is late."

"Late?"

Or missing. Max knew he couldn't dismiss the thought. With a murderer on the loose as well as a possible saboteur, he wasn't the only one wondering what was going to happen next. He held his breath as Pricilla stepped up to the mike. She'd done an outstanding job the past couple of days, but the stress of the contest was beginning to wear on all of them. With less than six hours of sleep, it was no wonder her voice didn't hold its normal spark of energy.

The sheriff leaned in toward him. "Has anyone checked his room?"

Max shrugged a shoulder as Pricilla addressed the audience, announcing the next segment of the competition. "I don't know. Apparently they called his cell phone, but he didn't answer. I don't know if anyone checked his room."

Sheriff Lewis crossed his ankles in front of him and frowned. "If I'd have known how much trouble this contest was going to cause, I'd have talked to the mayor himself about refusing to host it."

"I can hardly blame you."

The timer was set and the contestants jumped into action. With or without Freddie, it was apparent that the show would go on.

Even the contestants seemed to have taken on the sullen mood of the day. Their expressions were serious, and their normal interactions with the audience were gone. The audience responded with its own subdued silence.

Max watched as Michelle reached into her pocket for her cell phone. Moving back from the stage, she answered it and then stopped short before dropping her phone and collapsing in a heap onto the floor.

14

Freddie Longfellow is dead!" Sarah stood at the entrance
of the Great Room with a look of bewilderment across
her face.

Gasps from the audience followed her unexpected
announcement. Pans clattered in the kitchens. Something
crashed to the floor. For a full five seconds, no one moved,
including Pricilla. She'd expected further incidents of
sabotage but not another murder. Reality sank in, digging
deeper than a rooted tree. If Sarah was right and Freddie
was dead, the acts of sabotage had escalated—once
again—into murder.

Sending up a quick prayer for strength, Pricilla forced
herself to move across the stage to where Michelle lay.
Judging by her startled reaction, Pricilla could probably
delete the woman from her suspect list. Now if only she
could erase the fact that their murderer had just struck
again.

Surely there had been some kind of mistake.

A chair toppled over. Pricilla looked up. Apparently
she wasn't the only one who had jumped into action.
Sheriff Lewis barked into his radio for backup.

With Pricilla perched beside her, Michelle finally
started coming to.

Max bent over the two of them, casting a long shadow
from the stage lights. "Is she all right?"

"It must have been the shock of Freddie's death."

Or the probable end of the contest? Pricilla glanced up
at the camera that had stopped rolling. Another murder

might very well mean the canceling of the show. How many acts of sabotage was it going to take before the sheriff, or perhaps even the producers, nixed the show?

Which was, she was afraid, exactly what the murderer wanted.

Michelle groaned as she struggled to sit up. She pressed her hand against her forehead. "What happened?"

"You fainted."

"Fainted?" Her attempts to get up didn't work. "I've never fainted in my entire life."

The production manager joined the huddle. "I'm sorry to interrupt, but we're scheduled to be on the air and—"

"You're still on a commercial, right?" Pricilla asked.

"Yeah, but that only means that we're fine for another minute and a half or so. After that. . ."

Pricilla felt her joints protest as she rocked back on her heels. She'd been hired to introduce segments and interact with the audience, not make production decisions. She signaled to a burly cameraman for help. Michelle couldn't weigh over a hundred and twenty pounds, but there was no way she'd be able to lift the woman off the ground by herself.

"Did Sarah's announcement make it across the airways?"

The production manager shook his head. "I checked. She wasn't close enough to a mike for it to come through."

"Then get Sarah for me," she barked. She sounded like Michelle, but she didn't care. "Be ready to roll the cameras again as soon as the commercial break is over."

The manager jumped up to comply, while the

cameraman hoisted Michelle over his shoulder, despite her unladylike protests, and deposited her on a nearby chair.

Sarah came up, panting, out of breath. "He's dead, Mrs. Crumb. I saw him myself. It was the most horrible thing I've ever seen. He was just lying there beside his bed with blood across his face."

Fear—mingling with excitement—showed in Sarah's eyes. Did she see the incident as fodder for the book she'd written? Either way, now was not the time to stop and examine Sarah's motivation. If the show was to be saved, they needed to get Michelle back in commission. And she was going to have to focus enough that the television audience wouldn't find out that another murder had just taken place.

Pricilla closed her eyes and took a deep breath. "Sarah, get Michelle something to drink. Maybe some juice would be best."

"Of course."

Pricilla opened her eyes again and turned back to Michelle, who was now at least sitting up and looking halfway coherent.

"You didn't eat this morning, did you?" Pricilla questioned.

"A cup of black coffee. I. . .I didn't have time."

"Which would explain why you just passed out."

"I passed out because Sarah told me Freddie's dead. Can you even begin to realize what another murder is going to do to my show?" Michelle shook her head. "They're going to cancel the show, Mrs. Crumb."

The woman was actually more interested in going on with the show than in Freddie's death. Not a good

166 Chef's Deadly Dish

reflection of character by any means. But Pricilla couldn't worry about those implications. Not now, anyway.

"Forty-five seconds."

Pricilla groaned. Multitasking had never been her forte. How was she supposed to calm a distraught woman while at the same time run a live television show?

"I suppose that sounded heartless. I didn't mean it that way. . .not really." Michelle must have picked up on how she sounded. "It's just that I've been waiting for an opportunity like this for years."

Even Pricilla couldn't help but sympathize with her a little. "The sheriff's on his way upstairs now to see what's happened. In the meantime, there's been no mention of shutting things down."

"But we're down another contestant."

"You were planning to start without Freddie anyway—"

Michelle ran her fingers through her hair, which had lost its polished look. "They're going to fire me. Or at the very least, never let me produce another show again."

"No one's going to fire you. It's not your fault there's a murderer on the loose. And as you said before, any publicity is good publicity." Pricilla let out an audible sigh. Had she actually just said that?

The production manager hunched down beside them, addressing Pricilla. "We've got twenty more seconds until the commercials are over. Can you go on?"

Pricilla nodded. All she had to do was get through the scripted dialogue, and then the cameras would switch to the contestants in the kitchens. At least she wasn't on the hot spot that way. The poor remaining contestants were forced to think about cooking when another one of their colleagues had been picked off.

Pricilla took her place in front of the camera, waited for the red light, and forced a broad smile. "Good morning and welcome back to the third and final day of the Fifteenth Annual Rocky Mountain Chef Competition. . . ."

The room had been blocked off by the same yellow police tape Pricilla had seen in dozens of television shows. But seeing it in real life tended to put an eerie spin on reality. What was inside a person that could cause him or her to play God and take the life of another human being? The Bible said that money was the root of all kinds of evil, and if she was right, $250,000 had just sprouted into murder.

The sheriff stepped under the tape and joined her on the other side of the hallway. "Thanks for coming up here."

Max had agreed to let her go while he waited downstairs, but only because it was daytime and the hotel was crawling with officers of the law. "I've only got a few minutes until the next segment."

"That's all I need." He motioned inside the room. "I'd planned to bring Freddie in for questioning this morning. Don't have to do that now."

"No, you don't." Pricilla shuddered. The room was identical to hers, except for the lifeless body of Freddie Longfellow who lay motionless in the middle of the floor.

The sheriff tapped his hat against his thigh. "I'm considering canceling the contest."

"I can't say I blame you." Which was true, but the

other side of her gave in to the urge to convince him to save the show. "Except today's the last day. It would be a shame for all the contestants' hard work to be thrown away. And it's not as if the crime scene is downstairs in the kitchens."

"True, but the body count is already too high for my taste."

She stepped a bit farther down the hall, thankful her role in the case was only as an informal consultant and not anything that had to do with forensics. The small group in the room right now was brushing for fingerprints and searching for evidence.

All she had to search for was answers. Like what did Norton Richards and Freddie Longfellow have in common, besides the fact that they were now both dead? The prize money seemed to be the obvious common denominator. . . .

Pricilla cleared her throat and tried to stop her mind from wandering. "So what do you think? Is there a connection between the two murders, or are we looking at two completely different cases?"

The sheriff shook his head. "I wish I knew."

"How was Freddie killed?"

"The coroner will have to verify, but it looks like a blunt object to the head."

"Both could have been acts of passion."

"That's what I'm thinking. Maybe a confrontation. Someone trying to cover the tracks of the first murder."

"That would make the two crimes related."

"I'm going to need to talk to Maggie, and then to Lyle."

"Can you wait until the morning contest is over? They've all worked so hard to get to this point."

The sheriff let out a deep sigh. "I suppose it will take me that long to finish processing the crime scene."

Pricilla nodded her thanks. "What about Clarissa? Is she holding up?"

"Her parents will be here soon. I know that will be a boost to her spirits."

"You should tell her who you are. It's bound to come out once Judy shows up."

"The thought has crossed my mind more than once, but I don't know." The sheriff clasped his hands together. "I haven't seen her in twenty-odd years, and I thought I'd buried any feelings from the past."

"But you haven't, have you?"

He shook his head. "And now knowing that Judy will be here. . .I don't know. I guess it just dredges up things I'd just as soon forget. Clarissa has turned into a fine young woman without me. Maybe it's best to leave it like that."

"I don't agree."

"But Judy—"

"Judy will understand. And besides, Clarissa is a grown woman. She deserves to know the truth."

"I'll think about it. Right now I have another dead body to deal with, and I'm not sure we're any closer to finding the murderer."

Pricilla glanced at her watch. She'd be gone in another twenty-four hours. For Clarissa's sake, she had to find out who was behind this before then.

The sheriff called Pricilla's cell phone at half-past twelve to tell her that Judy and her husband, Bruce, had arrived and might need to see a familiar face if she was up to coming by the sheriff's office. While their distress over the situation was to be expected, they weren't, he informed her, taking the arrest of their daughter well.

With an hour and a half until the final session began, Pricilla kissed away any thoughts of an afternoon nap and headed with Max to the sheriff's office. Anything she could do for Clarissa would be worth a few more hours of lost sleep.

Clarissa's parents were sitting in the lobby of the sheriff's office when Pricilla and Max arrived. They were still dressed in shorts and a sundress more suitable for a Caribbean cruise than a holiday in the mountains. While Judy now wore her hair longer and had gained a few pounds, she'd changed little since Pricilla had seen her last.

Pricilla stepped up and gave her a welcoming hug. "It's good to see you, though I'm sorry the circumstances aren't better."

"I know. My little girl. . ." Tears poured down Judy's cheeks. "I can't. . .I can't. . ."

"Has she seen Clarissa yet?" While she was glad Clarissa's parents had finally made it here, seeing her mother hysterical wasn't going to help the already-tense situation.

Pricilla looked to the sheriff and Judy's husband. Both men shook their heads no.

Judy reached for a tissue from her handbag. "Martin—Sheriff Lewis—said I had to get ahold of myself first. That it won't do Clarissa any good to see me this way."

Pricilla squeezed Judy's hand and prayed that God would give her the words to say. "He's right, you know.

I know how hard it is, but you've got to be strong for Clarissa right now. Everything possible is being done to get her released, but until then. . ."

"I know you're right." Judy sniffled and then blew her nose again. "I just can't understand how this happened. Clarissa's never been in trouble before. Straight A in school, a hard worker—"

"None of that has changed. We're going to get her out." Pricilla glanced up at the two men. One who'd given life to Clarissa; the other who'd raised her as his own. Life wasn't always fair or easy. The past few days had more than proved that. "What Clarissa needs right now is for you to be strong. At least while you are in there with her. She needs to know that you can help her right now, especially when the system seems to be against her. Can you do that?"

Judy blew her nose and nodded.

"Good. Wipe your eyes, then go in there and just let her know you love her and that you'll stand by her through all of this no matter what happens."

Twenty minutes later Clarissa's parents emerged from the visitors' room. Judy's eyes were still red, but she'd stopped crying.

Pricilla stepped forward. "How is she?"

"Holding up. Somehow."

"And you?" Pricilla probed.

"Just praying that this nightmare will be over soon."

Judy stopped in front of the sheriff. "I want you to tell her who you are, Martin. She needs to know that you're on her side. I've never spoken ill of you, because what happened between us all those years ago was both our faults. Please, Martin. Do this for Clarissa."

Sheriff Lewis glanced at the door and shook his head. "I don't know. . . ."

Judy reached up and grasped his arm. "Please, Martin. She's a strong girl, but she needs all of us rallying around her. Do this for me. . .for her."

"I've just never been much for words. Put me in front of a group of officers or even a courtroom, and I know my place, but the daughter I haven't seen for over twenty years. . .I just don't know if I can do this."

"You can."

The sheriff turned to Pricilla. "You know her, Mrs. Crumb. Would you come with me to help her understand the situation?"

"Of course. If that's what you want."

Pricilla followed the lawman into the visitors' room. Clarissa sat in the same seat she had taken when Pricilla and Max had come two days earlier. Her face was still pale, but—perhaps because her parents were finally here—there was a spark of hope behind her eyes.

"Clarissa. . ." The sheriff stopped halfway across the room before moving to take a seat across from his daughter.

"Sheriff Lewis. Pricilla." Clarissa reached out and grasped Pricilla's hands. "Thank you for getting my parents here, Sheriff. You can't imagine what a relief it is just knowing they're in town now instead of somewhere outside the country."

Pricilla squeezed her hands. "I'm glad they're here as well. I know it's important."

Clarissa looked to the sheriff. "Please tell me you have good news about my case. It's been a nightmare for me, but now seeing what it's done to my parents. . .and I didn't even have anything to tell them."

"I wish I had something new to tell you."

Pricilla looked at Sheriff Lewis. "The sheriff does have news for you, but it's something. . .personal."

"Personal? I don't understand."

"You will. Just give him a moment to say what he needs to say."

The sheriff steepled his hands in front of him and took in a deep breath. Seeing them together, Pricilla noticed for the first time the striking resemblance in their reddish brown hair, blue eyes, and facial features. There was no doubt in her mind that Clarissa was his daughter.

"I'm not sure where to begin." He squeezed his eyes closed for a moment before continuing. "I used to know your mother."

Clarissa's eyes widened. "Wow. It's a small world."

"Clarissa, I don't know how else to say this than to simply say it. I'm Martin Lewis. Your mother's first husband and your. . .your biological father."

"My. . .my father?" Clarissa blinked, looking confused. "I know my mother divorced when I was a baby, but my father went back East. She never told me much."

"I worked in Philadelphia for a few years, then moved here to work with the sheriff's department."

"You're my father?"

Sheriff Lewis nodded.

Pricilla held her breath, wondering if another bomb-shell was going to be too much for the young woman to cope with. Another time, another place, maybe, but with a murder hanging over her head, maybe they'd all been wrong in thinking she needed to know about the sheriff now.

Clarissa's expression softened, relieving some of

Pricilla's fears. "I always wanted to know who my biological father was. Not that Bruce hasn't always treated me like his own daughter."

"I'm glad to hear that."

"You're my father," she repeated.

The sheriff nodded. "Your mother's kept me up-to-date from time to time on how you were doing. I'm so proud of you. You've become such a remarkable young woman."

"Why didn't you ever tell me? Ever try and contact me?"

"I. . .we thought it best. Bruce is your father."

"I wish I'd known. Just a photo. . ." Clarissa's gaze dropped. "I need to know something. Do you believe I'm innocent because you're my father or because you're a lawman?"

"Clarissa. . ."

"I need to know."

Sheriff Lewis's Adam's apple bobbed. "As your father, I know the kind of woman you are. Not one who would ever take the life of someone else. And as a lawman, I honestly believe that the evidence is going to prove your innocence in the end."

"And if it doesn't?"

His jaw tensed. "We'll all deal with that if we have to. In the meantime, I just want you to know I'm on your side, and I'll do everything I can to get to the bottom of who murdered Norton."

"Tell me what the DA is saying."

"Honestly?"

Clarissa nodded.

The sheriff swallowed hard again. "He's convinced that

we've arrested the right person. And unless new evidence turns up, there's a chance you will spend the next decade or two of your life in prison."

They were back to square one. Or so it seemed. Pricilla stood inside the lobby of the sheriff's office between Max and the lawman, wanting to make sure Sheriff Lewis was okay before she left. He grabbed a paper cup from beside the water cooler, filled it up, and then took a long drink.

"Are you going to be all right?" she asked.

Sheriff Lewis drew in a deep breath and nodded. "Believe it or not, I'm actually relieved. While it wasn't the meeting I've dreamed about for the past twenty-five years, at least my daughter knows who I am. And that I really do care about her."

"She's a grown woman now, and from the way things went, I'd say she's keen on the idea of further contact." Pricilla hoped her words were encouraging. "And the fact that you care about her enough to do whatever it takes to find out the truth will be worth something to her as well."

"But what if I can't?"

"There has to be a way." Pricilla fiddled with her purse strap. It was the lingering question none of them really wanted to face. "What about Freddie's death? Doesn't it prove Clarissa's innocent? If the two murders are related, then she couldn't have done it sitting in jail."

He crumpled the cup and tossed it into the trash. "The problem is that we still can't be certain that they are related. Or that she didn't have an accomplice who's still out there."

Max leaned against the wall and folded his arms across his chest. "Two murders occurring over the course of one weekend is a bit too much of a coincidence, don't you think? At least for them not to be related in any way?"

"I have to agree, but establishing exactly how they're related is what's proving to be the difficult part. Other than the fact that Clarissa was found over Norton's dead body, covered in his blood, I simply don't have any hard evidence. We still need something strong enough that will exonerate Clarissa completely. So far, with Freddie's death, we've found no real evidence leading to the perpetrator."

"What about the murder weapon?"

"Turned out to be the iron the hotel room provides, but it was wiped clean," the sheriff told her. "Apparently Freddie was pressing his chef's coat when the murder occurred. And because nothing appears to be stolen from the room, I believe it had to be an argument that escalated into murder."

"Did anyone see or hear anything?" Pricilla asked.

"No one that we've found so far."

Pricilla looked to Max. "Someone had to have heard something—"

"Pricilla?" Max asked. She knew exactly what he was thinking. One look at his frown told her that he'd had enough of her involvement in the case, especially after a second murder. And for once, she tended to agree. If only it weren't for Clarissa. . .

The brief reminder of Clarissa strengthened her resolve. "All I want to do is look around and ask a few questions."

"I think this time the sheriff should ask the questions. There's been another murder, Pricilla. It's not safe."

The sheriff nodded. "We'll continue to see if we can find a witness, but I believe that Max is right this time. The information you've managed to dig up has become an essential part of the investigation, but I don't want anything to happen to you."

Max reached out and squeezed her hand. "Me neither."

Max's smile made her forget what she was fighting for. Almost. The bottom line was that another man was dead, and Clarissa's future was still at stake—two things that she simply couldn't just ignore.

"I'll just keep my eyes and ears open," she conceded.

"No late-night treks though the hotel," Max told her.

"Or responding to any ruckus from outside," the sheriff added.

"Or—"

Pricilla held up her hand and laughed. "All right. I get the picture. I'll be careful. I promise."

Pricilla took another bite of her double-chocolate cheese-cake and swallowed a measure of guilt along with it. While Max had ordered a chef salad for lunch, she'd opted for a scrambled egg, bacon. . .and cheesecake. She couldn't help it. A bit of comfort food had suddenly become essential. And thankfully Max had been wise enough not to say anything.

"I feel as if we've hit a brick wall," she confessed.

Max dabbed another spoonful of dressing onto the rest of his salad. "The truth is going to come out eventually."

"But when? We're leaving in the morning."

"And Sheriff Lewis is perfectly capable of solving the case. Give him time." They were both silent for a moment while the waitress refilled their waters before moving on to another customer. "You still have a few minutes left to lie down before the last session if you'd like."

"Maybe I will." But when Pricilla glanced out the window, a glimmer of purple caught her eye near the shore, giving her second thoughts about a nap. "I think I'll take a short walk before the next session."

"A walk? Now?" Max glanced out the window, following her gaze.

"I won't go far. Just need to clear my head, and it's such a perfect day."

She quickly finished the last bite of her cake, hoping he wouldn't notice—

"Violet Peterson?" Max adjusted his bifocals and frowned. "Is that Violet Peterson?"

"Violet?"

"Pricilla, tell me something. Why is it you didn't invite me along on this walk?"

She cleared her throat. "There's nothing wrong with my taking a short walk. And if I happen to run into one of the contestants, or a member of the audience—"

"Or one of the judges." Max squeezed a lemon slice into his water and frowned. "What did we just finish discussing with the sheriff?"

"All I'm going to do is keep my eyes and ears open. Just like I promised."

"And what if Violet's the murderer?"

Pricilla matched his frown. "There are plenty of people around. If she was the murderer, she's not liable to try something in broad daylight when the lunch crowd is eating on the balcony above."

"I'm coming with you."

"I don't need a guardian angel, Max. I'll be fine. Really."

While she loved playing Sherlock Holmes alongside his Dr. Watson, something told her that Violet would open up better to her if she came alone. They didn't need to take any chances of intimidating the woman.

"You'd better get used to my role of guardian angel. Your habit of taking off without a thought about what could happen, well, take it from me, you need all the help you can get."

She decided to plead her case. "Max. I just think she'll respond better if it's just me. Woman-to-woman."

He hesitated before answering, clearly not agreeing with her reasoning. "Fine, I'll wait here, but don't be late. Michelle's going to hang you out to dry if you miss another session."

Pricilla glanced at her watch. "I'm not going to be late. I've still got another thirty minutes before I have to be back in the Great Room."

He leaned over and kissed her cheek. "The bottom line is that I love you, Mrs. Pricilla Crumb. Despite your stubborn ways—"

She kissed him on the lips to keep him quiet. "You know I love you, too, Max."

She made her way down the incline, hoping it would look as if she were out for a short walk along the shoreline and not looking for a chance to further a murder investigation. Violet stood at the shoreline in a purple-colored tailored pantsuit that looked more suitable for a boardroom than the mountains, even with the loaf of bread she carried to feed the ducks. A half dozen ducks had gathered around the middle-aged woman, thrilled with the free meal. But while she assumed that the city woman probably didn't know the difference between a trout and a bass, she definitely knew the intricacies of cuisine and how to run a business.

Pricilla approached Violet from the side, the lake spread out before them, shimmering beneath the early afternoon sun like hundreds of tiny crystals. The colorful array of columbines, poppies, Indian paintbrush, and a dozen other wildflowers only managed to add to the beauty she'd grown to love.

"It's stunning, isn't it?"

Violet tossed another piece of bread before turning to Pricilla. "Absolutely. I've been trying to figure out how I can arrange a month or two off so I can just sit out here watching the view. Maybe that would erase some of the stress of city life."

"I'd say your ducks look pretty carefree." One came up to Violet and nipped a morsel of bread from her fingertips.

"The only thing they have to worry about is where to get their next meal." Violet's laugh was light and contagious. "My father always gave me a loaf of bread to throw to the ducks back home. I loved to watch them gobble up the food I gave them. Life seems so simple when you're six."

Pricilla sensed the layer of sadness underneath her professional persona. "And today?"

Violet's smile withered. "After two murders and a contest that probably should be canceled? The world has turned into a complicated mess that's absolutely frightening to me. And that's not even taking into account the stress of normal everyday life."

Pricilla tried to gauge the woman's expression. She looked too genuinely upset, even scared, to be guilty. "At least it's almost over."

Violet sat down on the stone bench overlooking the lake. "As much as I really would love to hide out here for the next couple of months, I can't wait to jump on my plane tomorrow morning."

"I can hardly blame you. Do you mind if I join you for a moment?" Pricilla took a step closer. "I know we don't have much time, but I was hoping a bit of fresh air would help clear my mind."

"Not at all. I could use the company. I haven't wanted to be alone lately."

"I understand completely." Pricilla sat down beside her. There was nothing like a couple of murders to get you wanting to leave on the light at night.

"It's absolutely frightening, if you ask me." Violet threw out her last piece of bread and then wadded up the plastic bag. "I've seen you talking to the sheriff a number of times. You're not on his suspect list, are you?"

"His suspect list. . ." Pricilla shifted in the seat, taken aback by the question. Her relationship with the sheriff wasn't something she wanted to explain. "I'm working with him as a. . .a consultant."

The woman's eyes widened. "You mean a spy?"

"Well, that's not exactly the term I'd use."

Violet leaned against the back of the bench as if considering the idea. "That's not bad, actually. You're pretty much the one inside person, besides Michelle and maybe Sarah, I suppose, who can talk to both the contestants and the judges."

"And I've had some experience in working with the police." Pricilla paused before expanding on her exploits. Maybe she shouldn't have mentioned her past experience working with the authorities at all. It had never been on a professional level, and she had tended—to a degree anyway—to frustrate Deputy Carter more than help him, even though in the end her madcap escapades had eventually helped solve the cases.

"You've actually worked with the police? I'm quite impressed."

"It really isn't anything I like to brag about."

"Well, I have no idea how one might get involved in a murder investigation, so I say the more help, the better," Violet continued. "It frightens me knowing there's a murderer on the loose. I've judged contests before, but the worst thing that ever happened was missing ingredients, or maybe a refrigerator that wasn't keeping the correct temperature. There was no mention of murder in the contract I signed."

"I certainly agree with that." Pricilla decided to press further. "So you don't think Clarissa is guilty?"

"I don't know the girl, but she definitely didn't look like the murdering type."

"What does a murderer look like?"

"No one ever knows, I suppose, which is why I'd be willing to bet that Michelle's involved somehow. That woman will do anything for publicity."

"But murder?" Pricilla leaned in slightly. "That's an awfully strong accusation."

"Truth be told, Michelle's not the only one who once held a vendetta against Norton Richards. Besides, I'm not accusing, just observing."

"Anything specific?"

Violet shook her head. "I already told the sheriff I hadn't seen anything."

Maybe it was time for another angle. "I understand you knew Norton?"

"Knew him?" Violet fiddled with the plastic bag she still held between her fingers. "Hardly. I wouldn't have shaken hands with that man if my life depended on it. I've never understood where his popularity came from, and when I found out he was the substitute judge. . .well, you can understand my annoyance. Made me wish I could simply drop out."

"And your feelings toward him stem from a review he gave your restaurant?"

Violet looked surprised. "You heard about that?"

"I believe it was a review on your Coquille St. Jacques and stuffed mushrooms—"

"The man had some crazy agenda. He had to, to lie the way he did about my food. My restaurant has a solid reputation, which is something I've worked my entire professional life to uphold. Then he comes along and compares my cuisine to an overcooked microwave dinner." Violet's voice began to rise in volume. "You can imagine what that one negative review did for my reputation, after Norton Richards had the gall to waltz into my place like he was some sort of. . .of a god pronouncing judgment."

"I wouldn't go so far as to compare him to God."

"You get the point."

Pricilla forged ahead. "And you're sure that your staff wasn't just having an off night?"

It was obvious from Violet's wide-eyed expression that the question was insulting. "I have quality checks every step of the way to ensure my cuisine is top-drawer in every respect."

"Do you have any idea why he would give your restaurant such a negative review?"

"Of course I do."

Bingo. Pricilla hadn't expected such candidness, but maybe she was finally on to something.

"Which is. . ." she urged.

"Well, it's never been proven—and probably never will be now that Norton's dead—but it was never beneath him to use his power. And while I admit he found fame as a reviewer, he had always wanted to be a world-renowned chef—something he never achieved. So his fame became a poison dart he could throw at will to show he was still the one in control."

Pricilla crossed her legs. Clarissa had said nearly the same thing. Her boss, Jake, had been admitted into one of Europe's most prestigious cooking schools, but Norton hadn't been accepted. Grudges might run deep, as Clarissa had said, but there were still things that didn't add up.

Pricilla proceeded carefully. "What I don't understand is that a false review would, in the end, only serve to discredit Norton. Was it really worth the risk of his reputation?"

"Norton became more than just a reviewer. To the public, he was an icon who could do no wrong. If he said my Coquille St. Jacques tasted like a microwave dinner, then it tasted like a microwave dinner. That was simply the kind of power he held. Even so, I was in the process of suing him."

While she wasn't sure she would ever understand the hold Norton had once had on his readers, there was still one more question Pricilla wanted answered that could lead to a possible motive for Violet. "Was there ever any kind of settlement for you in the end?"

Violet shook her head. "I was hoping to have the whole thing over with this fall, but now that he's dead, there's no case."

Which meant that Norton's death would potentially cost Violet the settlement. Still. . .

"While it's sad the man is dead, most people I've talked to seem to believe that his death will work to their advantage."

Violet shook her head. "Not for me. I'll never be able to hear him apologize."

⁓

There were now four contestants left for the final session of the contest. Pricilla watched as Maggie Underwood, Christopher Jeffries, Brad Philips, and Gayle Wright worked feverishly in their kitchens to finish the final round of the contest. A task that for the moment, anyway, seemed to be anything but easy.

They had started five minutes late, and unfortunately, things had gone downhill from there. Pricilla studied the serious expressions of the contestants. Gone was the friendly interplay that had existed between the contestants and the audience. The spirited mood that had once filled the Great Room had now been replaced with a heavy sense of tension that was affecting the chefs' concentration.

Pricilla could feel the jumbled nerves. She'd bumbled over two lines in her script, and the audience had failed to laugh at her joke. Even Trisha's good news that her wedding dress was almost finished and their honeymoon reservations had been found had done little to lift Pricilla's spirits. All she could do for the moment was to paste on a smile when the camera rolled and pray she could keep it up until the red light went off.

For now Pricilla watched from the sidelines as the contestants worked to complete their last session, the Wild-card Dish. Ranging from elaborate desserts to sophisticated main courses, the chefs' goal during this segment was to blow away the judges—and the audience—with their unique creativity and style.

One of the cameras zoomed in on Christopher Jeffries, whose eyebrows were still noticeably singed from yesterday's explosion in his kitchen. His hands trembled as he set the top layer of his four-tiered cake. Pricilla gasped. Somehow he managed to save the triangular piece before it toppled off the side and onto the floor. But that lucky save couldn't be found for Brad Philips. The camera caught the chef pulling the hot water bath from his oven and then flipping it onto the floor. So much for his savory butternut flan appetizer. At this point Brad was more than likely out of the running. Hardly the grand finale they'd all hoped for.

The final bell rang, announcing the end of the wild-card segment. Pricilla let out a sigh of relief. All she needed to get through now was the formal award session that would be held later this evening.

Max joined her at the edge of the Great Room where she'd found a pot of hot coffee. "You made it through this afternoon."

"Barely." She took a sip of coffee that tasted more like her father's bitter campfire sludge. As long as it helped keep her awake. . . "Just remind me never to accept another honorary position as emcee."

He squeezed her free hand. "You've done terrific. Really."

"Maybe, but I can't tell you how relieved I'll be when all this is over. The tension in those kitchens this afternoon was thicker than this coffee."

The sheriff joined them, and Pricilla offered him a cup of the coffee. "I probably need it, but no thanks. I've been drinking so much coffee the past few days it's amazing I've gotten any sleep at all."

"Which is exactly what you need."

"You're probably right." The sheriff glanced across the room. Most of the audience had left, leaving only the crew to set up for the award ceremony. "I just received some news from the coroner I thought you might want to know."

"Good news, I hope?"

"At this point, I'm not sure how to interpret it."

'What do you mean?"

"The knife you pulled out of the lake. . .it wasn't the weapon that killed Norton Richards."

It took a moment for the sheriff's news about the knife to sink in. Pricilla had wanted the knife she found to be the murder weapon, because it proved—at least in her mind—that Clarissa was indeed innocent. Even the DA would have to agree that the girl couldn't have been in two places at once, a fact that was more than enough evidence for her.

"You're absolutely sure the knife wasn't what killed Norton?" Pricilla asked.

The sheriff took off his hat and nodded. "According to the coroner, that knife couldn't have made the wounds inflicted on Norton. They were a quarter inch too narrow and a half an inch too short."

Pricilla shrugged off her jacket and folded it over her arm. Even with all the overhead lights turned off, the room was still unpleasantly warm.

Max gripped her elbow. "Are you all right?"

"Honestly? No. I want this to be over."

She'd been so sure that the knife would be the evidence that threw out Clarissa's case and set her free. Hadn't the knife come from Clarissa's kitchen, meaning someone had recently thrown it into the lake? But why? She tossed the rest of her coffee into the lined bin and pondered the question. If it wasn't the murder weapon, what reason did anyone have to throw it into the lake in the first place? If it hadn't been for her jaunt with the metal detector to find Trisha's ring, the probability of anyone discovering the knife would have been next to nothing. It just didn't make sense. None of it.

A wave of fatigue swept over her. She slumped down into one of the extra chairs someone had lined up and leaned her head against the wall. If she could just close her eyes for five minutes. . .

"Pricilla?"

She caught the concern in Max's voice and opened her eyes again. "I'm fine. Really. Just tired after all that's happened here the past few days and frustrated that we're no closer to an answer."

Max didn't look convinced. "Why don't you go to your room and rest for an hour or two? You have plenty of time before the final session. Or we could go get something to eat first. Maybe that's what you need."

What she needed was for this to be over, for the real murderer to be behind bars instead of Clarissa. She sank deeper into the fabric-covered chair, surprised at how comfortable it was. Or maybe she was simply so tired anything would feel comfortable. "How about I meet you in the restaurant in a few minutes. All I need is a few minutes of quiet and I'll be fine."

"Alone?"

She grinned. The room was empty now, except for a couple of crewmen and one uniformed officer. "Max, I'll be fine." She looked at the sheriff. "Your guard isn't going anywhere, is he?"

"Stew will be here until this is over, and he knows I'll have his job if he leaves for any reason."

"See, Max. There's nothing to worry about."

Max still hovered in front of her. "All right, but don't be long. I'll be in the restaurant trying to avoid the coconut pie."

He spoke as if that fact would get her there faster. It probably would, but for the moment, Pricilla closed her eyes and took in a deep breath as the men walked away. The room still smelled like chocolate, something that normally would have been a temptation. But while the audience was enjoying samples of the chefs' creations in one of the other rooms, all she wanted to do was find a few minutes of escape without actually moving.

She pressed her fingers against her temples, hoping to ease the dull ache of her head. A second murder had underscored just how serious the situation really was and left her wondering if the murderer was finished.

I just don't understand any of this, God. It all seems so. . . wrong. Two men are dead, Clarissa's in jail. Why?

It all seemed to keep coming back to motive. Why kill Norton? Why frame Clarissa? Why kill Freddie in a fit of rage, if that's what it had been? Why were the answers to her questions continuing to be so elusive? She did know at least one answer. Sin had come into this world and, with it, pain and consequences. It had begun shortly after creation when Adam and Eve had to deal with the consequences of leaving the lush Garden of Eden and again when Eve must have asked God why He'd allowed Cain to kill her son.

Pricilla had asked God the same question when Marty died. The truth was that life was full of both pain and joy, and as the years had passed, she'd also learned the amazing truth that hard times stretched, polished, and strengthened. And joy could actually be found after tragedy. It was a reality that didn't always make sense. But one she knew to be true. Especially when God was in control.

Footsteps echoed beside her. Pricilla opened her eyes and then blinked.

Michelle had slid into the empty chair beside her. Flawless makeup, every hair in place, and not one wrinkle in her chic New York suit. How did the woman do it?

Michelle pulled her ever-present clipboard to her chest and grinned. "Well, Mrs. Crumb, we did it."

The fatigue had yet to lift. She should have gone upstairs like Max had suggested and slept for the next two hours. "We did what?"

"Finished the last session of the contest with a bang."

"A bang? I hardly see an almost-falling cake and splattered butternut flan as a triumph in the kitchen. I'd say every one of the contestants made at least one major mistake this afternoon, some of which were downright disastrous to their standings in the contest."

"That is true." The smile hadn't left Michelle's face.

"The pressure they face during a normal session with no problems is great enough," Pricilla continued. "Add a couple murders, sabotage, and a police investigation into the mix, and well, you saw them. They were all nervous wrecks."

Michelle's grin somehow managed to widen without drawing any lines across her face. Definitely Botox. "Don't you see? That's what made today's show so exciting. It's good television. Watching the chefs as they sweat over who will be taken in for questioning by the police next, all the while trying to create a masterpiece that will awe the judges. You just wait. Everyone will be tuned in tonight to see who will win the quarter of a million dollars—and to see who's left in the competition."

"That's horrible."

"Not at all. It's like Agatha Christie's famous book *And Then There Were None*. If she can make a story about people dropping like flies on some deserted island into a best seller, then I can make this contest, with its own reality-show mix of disappearing players, number one in the Nielson ratings."

Pricilla gasped at the woman's exuberance. If she had been in charge, the contest would have been canceled before it had even begun without a second thought as to whether or not they were wowing the audience or what the sponsors might think. It seemed to her that common decency and propriety should always come before reviews and good television.

Michelle leaned in slightly. "And by the way, the audience loves you as well. You add that homespun, grandmotherly charm to the show."

Pricilla coughed. Homespun and grandmotherly? She wasn't sure if thanks were due after that compliment—or whether or not it was even a compliment. "If you ask me, it's a pity that it took two tragedies to thrust the show into the limelight."

Michelle caught Pricilla's gaze. "Believe me, I agree that what has happened is horrid, but what's wrong with finding a bit of success in the midst of all this tragedy?"

Pricilla's eyes widened. "What's wrong with it? Two men are dead, Clarissa's in jail, and there is still both a saboteur and, even worse, a murderer on the loose."

Michelle clicked her tongue. "Like I said, good television."

Pricilla clenched the armrests of the chair before standing up, praying that she'd be able to keep herself from giving Michelle a tongue lashing—or worse. The younger woman didn't have a sympathetic bone in her entire body, and there was no doubt in her mind about one thing. If she had to choose from her list of suspects today, Michelle Vanderbilt would be number one on that list simply because, apparently, she had the most to gain from this string of disasters.

Pricilla stood to face Michelle. "I think it's sad, Miss Vanderbilt, when profit and prestige come before the respect and needs of people. God never intended us to treat each other this way, and your treating this as a spectacle, well, I believe it really breaks His heart."

"I'm not exactly into religion, Mrs. Crumb."

Pricilla shook her head. "I'm not talking about religion. I'm talking about treating people with respect and dignity, the way God intended. The problem with this world is that sin has taken over and trickled into every crack and crevice, and the only hope is realizing that Jesus' death on the cross is what can redeem each and every one of us. And if you ask me, this world could use a bit of redemption."

Michelle pushed her bangs back with a graceful swoop of her hands. "Do you really believe all that?"

Pricilla took in another long, slow breath. She hadn't intended on a sermon, but a deep frustration had taken over. God's laws weren't meant to be a bunch of mumbo-jumbo regulations to make life complicated and confining for mankind. They were made to bring life to His people. "Yes, I really do believe all that."

Michelle folded her arms across her chest. "How do you see me, Mrs. Crumb?"

"How do I see you?" Pricilla wasn't following.

The younger woman held up her hand. "Wait a minute, let me try. Driven, cold, and uncaring. Does that about sum it up for you?"

"Well, I wouldn't exactly. . ."

"Say those things out loud? That's okay, because I know you're thinking them. The thing is, sometimes that's what it takes to get ahead. And I'll do anything to get where I want to be."

Pricilla grabbed her jacket from the chair, poised to leave. "Even murder, Miss Vanderbilt?"

—

Pricilla rushed out of the Great Room and down the hall, wondering what had just happened. She'd once again practically accused Michelle to her face of murdering Norton Richards in order to up television ratings. A shiver ran down her spine. Surely even Michelle wasn't that coldhearted.

Or was she?

She pushed the button on the elevator and tapped her foot. If it wasn't for the awards ceremony, she'd be heading back to Rendezvous right now to the peace and quiet of Nathan's lodge. The bottom line was that Max was right. The sheriff could handle Clarissa's case better than she could, and the truth would eventually come out.

The elevator doors opened and Trisha stepped out in front of her. "Great news!"

She could use some good news at the moment. "What is it?"

"Riley just called. My dress is ready, and she wants me to come pick it up."

"That is wonderful news."

Trisha slung her purse onto her shoulder. "You'll come with me, won't you? It won't take long."

Pricilla hesitated. There was still time for her to lock herself in her room and take that nap, which would ensure not only that she felt more rested tonight, but that the bags under her eyes wouldn't be quite so obvious. Trisha's hopeful smile changed her mind. How could she even think about bailing on her soon-to-be daughter-in-law at this point?

"Of course, I'll come with you. I'll just need to let Max know that I'll be late for dinner." She glanced at her reflection in the mirror hanging on the wall before the doors closed, wondering if Botox wasn't such a bad idea after all. Her face looked pale, but at least her makeup still looked decent and her hair had a bit of bounce left. It would have to do. The last thing she intended to do was dampen Trisha's spirits. "Let's go."

—

Fifteen minutes later, Riley opened the front porch door of her log cabin-styled house before either of them had the chance to ring the bell. Wearing jeans and a purple T-shirt, she welcomed them in and led them through the veranda to the entrance of the older home.

"You'll have to excuse the mess. I just haven't had time to keep up with everything."

Trisha laughed. "I suppose that's my fault, keeping you so busy with my dress."

"Oh, I love every minute of the sewing, but these past few months have been extra busy."

Pricilla stepped around a table piled with unopened fall magazines, junk mail, a small FedEx box from Sally's Scissors Emporium, and two empty boxes of Froot Loops.

She followed Riley into the house, which wasn't any cleaner. While the woman had a way with design and sewing, her housekeeping skills were on a completely different level altogether. The two couches in the living room were covered with laundry, newspapers, and magazines. And it appeared as if no one had eaten at the dining room table for months. It was covered with books and an assortment of dishes and knickknacks.

"I would have dropped the dress off at the lodge myself, but I'm running behind. I'm supposed to leave tonight for Denver."

Pricilla tried to ignore the mess without tripping over any of it as she crossed the gold shag carpet and continued down the long hallway. "Your next job?"

"Six bridesmaid dresses plus an antique wedding gown complete with ten yards of lace, an eight-foot train, and two hundred pearl buttons."

Pricilla let out a low whistle. "You really do have your work cut out for you."

"According to the bride, they found the patterns in her grandmother's cedar chest. She decided to recreate the vintage look and go for a truly old-fashioned wedding."

"So you're not going to make it to the awards ceremony tonight?"

"For the contest?" Riley stopped in front of one of the closed bedroom doors and shook her head. "I've got something to do before I leave town, but even if I was going to be around, I have no desire to watch someone win $250,000. It's a bit ridiculous, don't you think? I've always wondered why school teachers make minimal salaries while sports stars and movie stars—and apparently chefs—are paid a fortune to look good in front of the camera."

Funny. Pricilla had been paid to look good in front of the camera and promote the contest, but somehow she'd missed out on the fortune part.

Trisha peeked inside the room. "Can I see the dress before we leave, or do you have it wrapped up?"

"I thought you might want to see it, so I left it out in the back room." Riley motioned them toward the other end of the hallway.

Pricilla walked past another closed door and then an open one that must have been Riley's bedroom. A large red suitcase halfway packed with clothes was open on top of the queen-sized bed, and the floor was covered with more clothes, making it as bad as the living room. On the walls of the hallway were a half dozen photo collages.

Pricilla stopped for a moment to study them.

One of Riley's parent's restaurant, The Krab Kettle, caught her eye. Riley, who had changed little in the past few years, stood smiling between a woman who looked enough like her to be a sister, and a rotund young man with glasses. There was something familiar about his eyes, but she couldn't place him. Perhaps someone she'd met at the lodge. . .

"Family photos?" she asked.

"Yeah. My mother never could get rid of any of them. The dress is this way." Riley herded them down the hall toward the back of the house. "Sorry, I'm in such a hurry."

Pricilla brushed past the rest of the photos, wishing she had a few more minutes to study them.

While the entire house required a visit by Britain's own *How Clean Is Your House?* duo, Riley's sewing room was crowded but neat. How was it that some people could be organized in one area and a complete disaster in another? She'd never understand.

The sewing room, though, would be any seamstress's dream. From the sewing table and machine, to the shelves full of fabrics, threads, and other sewing notions all arranged by color and function, the contrast to the rest of the house was enormous.

"What a wonderful work space."

"It is great, isn't it—though what I wouldn't do for a proper store where I could hire a couple assistants and work full-time. The problem is that this town can't support me. There will simply never be enough business."

"What about Denver or some other large city? You've got the talent to make yourself known in a place like that." Pricilla studied the penciled dress designs on the large table, impressed with the uniqueness in Riley's style. "I've done my own fair share of sewing and tailoring, and my talents don't run near your level."

Riley laughed, her impatience apparently forgotten. "Who knows? Maybe one day I'll give the big city a try. For now, though, I can't complain too much. I have plenty of work, and the location isn't too bad, either."

Trisha's wedding dress hung on the far side of the room. Pricilla crossed the wood floor and ran her finger down the smooth fabric, impressed at the intricate details Riley had added. The beaded handwork Trisha had asked for was now complete and ran across the bodice in simple lines trailing down the front.

Riley pulled an extra-large garment bag from the closet and began unfolding it on the worktable. "So the two of you are leaving in the morning?"

"Bright and early," Trisha responded. "And I have to

say, I've never been so ready to leave a place as I am this one."

Riley looked up from the table. "Because of Norton's death?"

"I guess you haven't heard the latest news from the lodge." Pricilla helped the younger woman lay out the bag they'd used to cover the dress.

"No, I've been here all morning and haven't heard anything. Didn't even turn on the television."

Pricilla dropped the edge she'd been holding. "There's been another murder."

"Another murder. . ." Riley's face paled. "You can't be serious."

"Unfortunately, she is," Trisha said.

Riley shook out the bag and began to unzip it. "So what do the police think? That there's some crazed serial killer on the loose?"

Trisha shrugged. "I suppose that could be one explanation."

"I doubt it's a serial killer," Pricilla began, "though the police still have no idea who's behind things."

"So they think it's the same killer?"

"There's obviously a bit of discrepancy on that one," Pricilla said. "Clarissa's still in jail, even though there is no way she could have murdered both men."

The room was silent for a moment. "Who was killed?"

"One of the contestants," Trisha told her. "Freddie Longfellow."

"Longfellow. And the police don't have any leads?"

"Not yet."

"Maybe it's a good time to leave town then." Riley

lifted Trisha's dress down off the hook. "Living alone, I certainly don't like the idea of staying around with some crazed murderer on the loose."

Trisha nodded. "I agree completely."

"So who do you think the killer is, Mrs. Crumb?"

"Honestly? I'm not sure at this point. Norton had a bone to pick with everyone. But Freddie, his death adds a twist to the entire situation that I just don't know how to decipher. The man was a bit too cocky in my opinion, but that's certainly not a reason to kill someone."

Riley shivered. "Somebody obviously had a reason."

Ten minutes later, Pricilla and Trisha left with the dress lying neatly in the backseat of the car.

Trisha glanced at it. "I admit that the dress was a bit of an extravagance, even when I first bought it, but Riley transformed it into a masterpiece."

"I'm so glad you're happy with it. It is beautiful."

"How much time do we have until the next session?" Trisha asked from the passenger seat.

Pricilla glanced at her watch. "We're fine. I've got forty-five minutes until I have to be there."

"Good."

Pricilla took the sharp turn toward the lodge and felt the car shudder beneath her. She pressed the brake, fighting not to run into the ditch that ran along the side of the road.

Trisha grasped the armrest as Pricilla finally came to a complete stop. "What's wrong?"

Pricilla glanced in the side mirror and smacked her hands against the steering wheel. "Look's as if we've got a flat tire."

Pricilla stepped out of the car to examine the back tire and groaned at the shredded tread. She'd been right. The tire was flatter than her aunt Bell's infamous creamed corn soufflé. The woman never had been able to cook. And Pricilla had never changed a tire. Three miles from the nearest town on a narrow gravel road made that reality even more serious. At least they had a cell phone.

"A flat tire?" Trisha came around the back of the car, stopped abruptly, and then let out a low whistle. "You weren't kidding, were you?"

"I wish I were." Pricilla struggled to formulate a plan while trying not to worry about what Michelle would say about this latest excursion—especially if Pricilla was late for the contest's last session. "You know Michelle's going to kill me if I'm late."

Trisha rested her hands on her hips and frowned. "Not a very appropriate cliché to use considering all that's happened the past few days."

"True, but that doesn't change the fact that if I don't show up on time for the final awards ceremony, Michelle will be furious."

Pricilla started to lean against the side of the car, stopping when she noticed the layer of dust that would end up on her pale yellow skirt. She needed to show up on time and as smudge-free as possible.

"Let's not worry yet." Trisha started digging in her purse and pulled out her cell phone. "Nathan can be here in less than ten minutes, which means we'll be back in plenty of time for you to change."

Pricilla glanced at her watch. "I've got thirty-five minutes and counting."

Granted, thirty-five minutes of worrying wasn't going to do anything but add to the stress of the weekend, which definitely wasn't worth it. All they needed to do was call Max and Nathan who could in turn worry about getting the tire changed—after they rushed her back to the lodge.

"Pricilla. . ." Trisha held the phone up above her head and frowned.

"What is it?"

"A problem. There's no signal."

Pricilla felt her blood pressure rise. "There's got to be a signal."

"We are out in the middle of nowhere." Trisha dropped the phone back into her purse and eyed the tire. "You do know how to change a flat, don't you?"

Pricilla cocked her head and stared at the black mess of rubber. "Sort of."

"Sort of? It was a simple yes or no question!"

"I learned how to. Once. My father made me take an auto mechanics course in college."

"Which was. . ."

"Forty-five years ago, give or take."

Trisha folded her arms across her chest. "You're joking, right?"

"No." Pricilla eyed the tire again, wishing she was joking.

"And you don't remember how?"

"You take off the screws, then jack up the tire. . ." Pricilla caught her lower lip between her teeth. "Or is it the other way around. . ." She glanced up and caught Trisha's gaze. "Nope. Not a clue. What about you?"

"Somehow I missed that lesson in driver's ed."

"You missed that lesson?" This couldn't be happening. "Where's my ever-reliable, independent, soon-to-be daughter-in-law?"

"It rained the day we were supposed to take How to Change a Tire 101. Besides, up until now, I've never needed to change a tire. Back in New Mexico, I'd simply call a tow truck."

"Something we can't do considering we don't have any phone service."

"True."

"Then it looks as if we have two options at this point," Pricilla began. "One, we can attempt to change the tire, or two, we can start walking. We're about halfway between town and the lodge, so you can even take your pick which direction, though I'd prefer at least walking in the direction of the lodge so I can feel as if I'm making progress."

"I would normally agree, but. . ." Trisha looked down at her two-inch heels, which looked great with her dark jeans and her short-sleeved green sweater, but weren't made for an impromptu walk down a gravel road. "You don't have a third option? One that doesn't include a hike down a deserted road in heels?"

Pricilla looked down at her own shoes, thankful she'd opted for the tan flats and not the brown heels. "You do have a point, but so far I haven't come up with a door number three."

Trisha's gaze dropped to the ground. "There is another problem to consider as well. The fact that there have been two. . ."

Trisha stopped before finishing her sentence, but she didn't have to for Pricilla to know exactly what she was thinking about.

Murder.

She shuddered. "Two murders? I know. I've been thinking the same thing."

Pricilla glanced at the tire again. Not that she thought her car had been sabotaged, or even that there was any chance that the murderer could be out here, but there was something unnerving about being out on a lonely road after having to deal with not one, but two unsolved murders.

Pricilla worked to shake off the eerie feeling. "If you can think of another option, I'm up for trying."

Trisha eyed the tire again. "We could try to change it. How hard can it be?"

"Forget it." They spouted the words in unison and then laughed, easing the tension slightly.

"Okay then." Trisha slung her purse over her shoulder. "You know we're being silly, really. It's not as if we're hitchhiking after dark. We merely need to make it back to the lodge, which is only a couple miles from here. It'll be a snap."

Pricilla did a quick calculation in her head. If they walked an average of four miles an hour, she might make it in time, though she could forget about freshening up and changing clothes. This was definitely going to be her last time in front of a camera.

Pricilla locked the car and tried to find a bright side of the scenario as they started walking toward the lodge. "Look at it this way. We now have time to brainstorm the murders."

"Brainstorm the murders?" Trisha shook her head. "That's not exactly the topic I was wanting to dwell on."

Pricilla swerved to the right to avoid a large rock, wondering just how long her semicomfortable flats would make it on this terrain, let alone Trisha's heels. "We could discuss the appetizers and floral arrangements for your wedding."

Trisha hobbled alongside her. "But you'd much rather discuss a whodunit."

"Only because I've got just over twelve hours before I leave, and I intend to make some headway in finding the truth before then."

"I know you believe Clarissa's innocent, but didn't the sheriff say you needed to stay out of the investigation? Another murder is serious business, and I, for one, have no desire to get involved in it."

"You sound just like Max," Pricilla countered. "I promised to stay out of trouble, which I intend to do—to the best of my ability. But I also promised Clarissa I'd do everything I can to help get her free, which means that until I have to leave, I intend to do exactly that."

Along the road, golden leaves from the trees danced in the light breeze beneath the shadow of the Rockies. Clean mountain air, the warm sun on her face, and a mountain jutting up above them. . .she should be enjoying it, not worrying if there was a murderer on the loose.

Trisha shoved her hands into her back pockets. "So who's at the top of your list?"

"Twelve hours ago, Freddie Longfellow was right at the top."

"Who just took himself out of the running this morning."

"I'd much rather be a suspect than a dead victim."

"True," Trisha admitted. "And I'm sure Freddie would wish that as well if he were still alive."

Pricilla glanced down at Trisha's shoes. They had to be uncomfortable. Barely half a mile down the road and her own feet were already starting to ache.

"What about now?" Trisha asked. "Anyone surfaced to the top of your list?"

"Michelle's the first person that pops into my mind."

But while it was true that Michelle had both motive and opportunity, Pricilla had learned that things weren't always as they seemed. She wished there were a convenient way to study the printouts Max had given her. Seeing the suspects and their motivations laid out side by side helped tremendously in organizing her jumbled thoughts.

Instead, Pricilla shook her head and let out a long sigh as they turned right at the fork in the road and started uphill. She was beginning to sound like a genuine sleuth, instead of the formerly retired chef and soon-to-be-grandmother—she hoped—that she was. No. She should be reading whodunits instead of trying her hand at solving murders like some escapade from Agatha Christie's Miss Marple books. Murder was police business, as Max was always quick to remind her, and the bottom line was, he was right.

The only problem was that not getting involved in a situation where she was needed had never been her strong suit. And Clarissa definitely needed her.

"Michelle had motive and opportunity," Pricilla finally continued, feeling breathless. With the uphill incline increasing, her lungs gasped for air. "And she doesn't have an alibi, according to Sarah. Add to that that she's lied—or at least withheld information—about several key situations."

Trisha was starting to limp slightly. "From outside appearances, Michelle seems to have enough motivation and drive to bend the rules and to get exactly what she wants."

Including murder? The same question continued to surface. Pricilla hoped not, but someone who was obviously driven by something had killed both Norton and Freddie.

"I'm afraid you're right about Michelle."

"Mom?" Trisha's voice came out like a squeak a few steps behind her.

Pricilla spun around. Trisha was standing on the side of the road, bent over. "What's wrong?"

Trisha slipped off her shoe. "The heel just snapped off."

"You're kidding."

She held up the broken piece. "I wish I was."

"Well, you can't go barefoot. This road is full of gravel."

Trisha pulled off the other shoe.

"What are you doing?"

"If I can break off the other heel, at least I won't end up throwing my back out of whack by walking unevenly on this surface."

Trisha fought to break off the heel. Nothing. She bent down and whacked it against a large rock.

"It's not working." She struck it against the rock again and then quickly drew back her hand. "Ouch!"

"Trisha—"

"I'm fine." Trisha groaned. "I just managed to bash

my finger along with my shoe. So much for my Elizabeth Long originals."

"Expensive?"

Trisha laughed. "Twenty-five bucks on sale."

"It looks as if we're back to option *A*."

"Limping back to the lodge."

Trisha started off at a brisk, lopsided shuffle. "This is nuts, you know. Hiking back to the lodge in a pair of mismatched heels with a murderer on the loose. I should write a book about all that's happened this weekend."

"Let's just hope this story has a happy ending," Pricilla added.

At the moment, a happy ending included getting back to the lodge in time to change and freshen up before she was due in front the camera. She glanced at her watch and quickened her pace. They were down to twenty-five minutes before Michelle expected her and at least another two miles. She was never going to make it.

Trisha, still struggling to keep up, pulled out her cell phone again.

Please, Lord. . .

"Anything?" Pricilla asked after a moment.

"Nothing." Trisha shook her head, dumping the phone back into her purse. "There is a bright side to all of this."

"A bright side?" Pricilla wasn't convinced.

"We're walking off some of the calories from the weekend."

Pricilla chuckled. "You do have a point, but right now I'd prefer the extra pound or two to this."

Gravel crunched behind them. Pricilla turned around. Maybe they would get a ride to the lodge after all. She shielded her eyes from the setting sun with her hand and caught a glimpse of Michelle's red sports car, top down. She pulled up alongside them and crawled to a stop.

Great. Pricilla bit the edge of her lip. How was it that their one ticket back to the lodge was also her number-one suspect?

Trisha was the first to speak. "Oh, Michelle, I can't tell you how glad we are to see you."

Pricilla wasn't quite as convinced. Obviously the opportunity to avoid walking back to the lodge with a broken shoe far outweighed any fears Trisha might have that they might be catching a ride from a murderer.

Michelle smiled. "Well, well. It seems as if my favorite emcee and her sidekick have once again managed to find themselves in yet another predicament. How do you do it, Mrs. Crumb?"

Pricilla shook her head. The woman didn't have a sympathetic bone in her entire body. "We had a flat tire."

"Yes, I passed your car just now. So there were no metal detectors or sabotage involved?"

"Sabotage?" Trisha threw Pricilla a concerned glance.

"Of course not," Pricilla said, dismissing the idea. She wasn't going to let the woman scare her. Her imagination had done enough running for the day. Which meant it was time to change the subject. "You wouldn't by chance happen to know how to change a tire, would you, Michelle?"

"Change a tire?" Michelle shifted her car into park. "This suit cost five hundred dollars, which means even if I did know how to change a tire, I wouldn't. I'm sure the lodge will be able to send someone to change it for you."

Trisha dangled her broken heels behind her. "Then

would you mind giving us a ride?"

"Of course not. Jump in, and I'll drive you both back to the lodge."

Pricilla hesitated as an eerie sensation brushed over her. If Michelle were the killer, that meant. . . No, she was definitely overreacting. Just because she had motive, opportunity, and means didn't automatically mean she was guilty. She was simply being helpful. They had nothing to worry about.

Pricilla must have hesitated too long, because Michelle leaned over to pop open the front passenger side door. "Come now, Mrs. Crumb. You look as if you've seen a ghost. Surely you don't really think that I killed Norton, or Freddie, for that matter. Is that the problem?"

"Of course she's not worried." Trisha had already climbed into the backseat of the immaculate convertible and had a smile on her face. Apparently she had forgotten that they were about to get into the car with their number-one suspect.

Pricilla winced as a wave of guilt washed over. She was being unreasonable, but she couldn't help it. This probably wasn't the time for a bit of sleuthing, but. . . "To be honest, Michelle, you do have motive for at least Norton's death."

"Something you've made quite clear. And so do half the contestants and judges," Michelle quipped.

"She has a point." Any traces of fear had left Trisha's voice. The chance for a ride back to the lodge had obviously pushed her over to the other side. "Come on and get in, Mom. After all your worries about being late, we're actually going to make it."

"I'll even make a deal with you, Mrs. Crumb,"

Michelle said as Pricilla gave in and climbed into the car. "Ask me anything you want, and I'll give you an answer."

"An honest answer?"

"I didn't say that, but, yes, an honest answer. Then maybe, just maybe, you'll finally agree with your future daughter-in-law that I'm not the horrid monster you think I am."

"I never said—"

"One question, Mrs. Crumb." Michelle pulled back onto the narrow road and continued on to the lodge. "Any question."

"Okay. Where have you been? The final award segment of the contest starts in less than an hour, and we're supposed to be there thirty minutes before that. I expected you to be rushing around making sure everything was in place by this time."

"I had a business appointment. Sarah can handle things without me for the moment."

"Who was the meeting with?"

"The deal was one question, Mrs. Crumb."

"True, but. . ."

Michelle clicked her cherry red nails against the matching steering wheel. "But I'm feeling generous. I had a meeting with the man you saw me with at the pharmacy."

"So you did know him."

"I presumed you figured that one out, so call it a freebee. I suppose it was a strange place for a meeting."

At the local pharmacy? You could say that.

"Then you don't mind explaining," Pricilla probed.

"Yes, actually. I do mind. It was a personal matter that has no bearing at all on the sheriff's murder investigation.

Which is, I assure you again, the truth."

"Okay. I suppose it is your business."

"Yes, it is."

The only sound for the next few moments was the wind rustling through the open convertible. Michelle's short hair flew in every direction, but she didn't seem to mind. No doubt, like her perfectly made-up face and elegant, unwrinkled suit, once they returned to the lodge, her hair would automatically fall perfectly back into place. Pricilla's own short curls, on the other hand, would take a miracle to tame before she stood in front of the camera again.

"Can I ask you a question now, Mrs. Crumb?" Michelle's question broke the silence.

"I suppose." Pricilla squirmed in her seat and pressed her fingertips against the cherry red leather interior that had to have cost a pretty penny. Michelle might be fighting for a prime-time spot in front of the cameras, but she was still obviously doing well financially.

"You've been pretty chummy with the sheriff these past few days," Michelle began.

"I've been. . ." Like with Violet, Pricilla paused, once again wondering just how much information she should offer. Clearly, though, her interaction with the sheriff these past few days hadn't gone unnoticed. "I've been helping him as a sort of consultant. In an unofficial capacity, of course."

"She solved two murders back in Rendezvous this past year," Trisha piped up from the backseat.

"You're kidding."

"Unofficially, of course," Pricilla clarified again. "I just happened to be in the right place, or shall we say the wrong place, at the right time, and was able to help."

"I thought amateur detectives were only found in mystery novels and maybe a rerun of *Murder, She Wrote*," Michelle said.

"Like I said, it's all been informal and completely unofficial."

"So here's my question. Where am I on Sheriff Lewis's list of suspects? You must know."

Pricilla noted the woman's stern profile. Her normal confidence had rapidly melted into something that sounded like pure fear.

"To be honest, I don't know," Pricilla confessed. "The sheriff doesn't let me know everything regarding the case. He just has looked to me for insight on things I might pick up by being part of the competition."

Michelle took her foot off the accelerator as they went over a couple of large bumps in the road. Pricilla drew out a sigh of relief. In another couple of minutes, they'd be back at the lodge.

"Then maybe you can tell him this," Michelle said. "I've worked hard, made some mistakes, and taken advantage of opportunities, and in the process stepped on a few toes, but I never killed anyone. And I didn't kill Norton."

"Is that what you're afraid of? That the sheriff is going to arrest you for murdering Norton?"

"Wouldn't you be afraid if you were me? I know what it looks like. Not only do I have motivation and opportunity, I panicked and didn't tell the sheriff about my relationship with Norton." Michelle gripped the steering wheel until her knuckles turned white. "We. . .we had an affair a few years ago."

"I know."

"You know? Then I can assume that the sheriff knows as well."

"He knows that you've been covering up some things, including the affair. But whether or not he's planning to arrest you, I don't know."

"People are so predictable, it's scary."

"What do you mean?"

"Have you heard of Brandt Watson?" Michelle sped past a grove of aspen trees whose yellow leaves dripped like gold from the white limbs.

"Brandt Watson?" Pricilla shook her head. "I don't think so."

"He was a famous outlaw back in the late eighteen hundreds from this part of the country, though there are a few people who believe he was actually a hero. He was worth over a million dollars when he died."

"And what does that have to do with us today?"

"It's interesting how things are," Michelle continued, not answering Pricilla's question directly. "You get ahead and people assume you did it in some unscrupulous fashion. Newspapers print the sensational, filling in what they want between the lines, and sometimes, out-and-out lying. It was that way with Brandt Watson. People saw him with his money and power and found it easier to believe that he'd gained wealth by some sort of evil deeds instead of hard work. And do you know what? People are exactly the same today as they were back then."

"So he wasn't an outlaw?"

"Oh, no. He earned his money the old-fashioned way. A lot of hard work and a bit of luck."

"How do you know?" Trisha asked.

"Brandt Watson was my great-grandfather on my mother's side."

Pricilla began to see where Michelle was going. "And the same thing has happened to you?"

"Did you know that last year I was arrested for assaulting one of my colleagues? Marcy Lee knew I was up for a promotion and wanted it. She deliberately picked a fight with me, knowing my temper would get the better of me. Then she brought a lawsuit against me, claiming I had "harassed" her. She almost won her lawsuit and the promotion, but they finally had to drop it because it was her word against mine."

"Why'd she do it?" Trisha asked.

Michelle continued down the bumpy road that was flanked by purple wildflowers on either side. The sun had already dropped behind the mountains, leaving the horizon a hazy band of orangish yellow.

"Isn't that obvious? Marcy wanted the promotion and figured that the easiest way to get it was to get rid of me."

"But none of her accusations were true?"

"Oh, we had a fight, but I never struck her. In the end, though, it didn't matter because I was still made out to be the bad guy in some people's eyes. Innocent or not. I managed to get the promotion but learned in the process that you can't get ahead by being Mr.—or Miss—Nice Guy."

"So why are you telling us this?" Pricilla asked.

"Because I'm tired of the lies and rumors and gossip. I'm tired of working hard, only to be snubbed because people perceive me as some kind of hatchet woman. I've gotten promoted by hard work and sweat. I'm always the first one at the office, and by the time the rest of them show up, I've already put in a half-day's work."

While Pricilla was certain Michelle would never admit it, Pricilla could hear the deep hurt in the younger woman's voice. "It's called being driven, Michelle, something that can be a positive quality. But sometimes that drive can be the very same force that ends up running over people. And in the end, you're the one who ends up feeling isolated and alone."

Michelle's chin jutted out. "So then I'm the one who suffers, because I'm driven and disciplined?"

"Sometimes."

"Maybe they're right."

"Who's right?" Pricilla asked.

"I've heard the names they call me. Ice Woman. Heartless. Cold-blooded." Michelle shrugged, looking more deflated than Pricilla's back tire. "But it doesn't mean I don't have any feelings. And now everyone has taken those old rumors and twisted them once again. The truth is, Marcy Parks didn't have the drive it takes to become what she wanted, so she decided to take me down any way she could. Nobody wants to hear the truth. They would rather hear that I socked a woman in order to get ahead.

"And you know what else I'm tired of?" she continued without hardly taking a breath. "People assume things about me before they even know me. Men don't want to date me because they're threatened by me, and women don't want to befriend me because they're jealous. Yet I've worked my way up from living on a shoestring to. . ." She held her hand up. "To this."

Pricilla looked around at the car, the expensive suit, and the manicured nails and knew that one thing was true. "But you still want more, don't you?"

Michelle's laugh rang hollow. "Who doesn't?"

"In the end, it's all meaningless, Michelle. Nothing more than a chasing after the wind."

"So you're back to your religion again?"

"Are you happy with all this, Michelle?"

There was no response as they passed the carved sign announcing the Silvermist Lodge in half a mile, which made Michelle's answer clear. Pricilla hadn't missed the sadness in the young woman's gaze or the loneliness.

Michelle turned and caught Pricilla's eye. "Do you still want to know whether or not I killed Norton?"

"Did you kill him?" Pricilla asked. She didn't like the way the conversation had abruptly switched, but she needed to know.

Michelle swung the car around and headed back toward town.

"What are you doing, Michelle?"

"Pricilla?" Trisha spoke up from the backseat.

"Michelle, I'm not sure that now is the time to show me whatever it is you want to show me. We need to get back to the lodge."

Michelle stepped on the gas. "Don't worry, Mrs. Crumb. What I have in mind won't take long at all."

18

Max sat at the table waiting for Pricilla—something he'd been doing a lot of lately, it seemed. Not that he minded waiting for her, but he was hungry, and the water the waitress had brought him had done little to curb his appetite. He glanced at the menu, wondering if they'd have time to even order. The restaurant was busy and the awards ceremony was supposed to start in less than an hour. He could always order an appetizer to hold him over until she arrived, but if she wasn't here in the next few minutes, there wasn't going to be time for her to eat.

As if she could read his mind, the waitress reappeared at his table. "Can I get you something else until your party arrives?"

Max eyed the list of options, debating between a side salad and hot wings.

Charlotte, as her name tag read, flipped open her order pad. "The appetizer special for tonight is crab stuffed mushrooms in a rich butter sauce."

Butter sauce. Even better. Max tapped his fingers against the table. Pricilla would tell him that it was off limits, but in his defense this was their last night here. It couldn't hurt. Not really.

"I'll take one order of the stuffed mushrooms and a refill on my water."

"Coming right up."

She skirted away from the table and barely missed knocking into Nathan who'd come up behind her.

"Excuse me." Nathan spoke to the waitress as he slid

into the seat across from Max. "Sorry I'm late. Where are the women?"

"I was about to ask you that." Max glanced toward the entrance of the restaurant. "They're not with you?"

"I thought Trisha said she'd meet me in the lobby between five and five thirty. Maybe I misunderstood her." Nathan shook his head. "Or we've both forgotten that they've gone to pick up my bride-to-be's wedding gown."

Max laughed. "Which explains a lot. Three women and a wedding dress. . ."

Nathan pulled his cell phone from his shirt pocket. "I'm sure there's nothing to worry about, but I'll still give Trisha a call. Too many strange things have happened this weekend."

A sliver of guilt sliced through Max as Nathan made the call. He should have gone with them to pick up the dress. The only reason he hadn't offered was because Pricilla already thought he was being too protective. But when had things like chivalry and gallantry become passé?

Nathan flipped his phone shut. "There's no answer. They must be out of range."

"I'm sure there's nothing to worry about."

"No. Nothing to worry about at all."

The waitress set Max's appetizer on the table and took Nathan's drink order before leaving. Max glanced at the plump mushrooms piled on the plate. His appetite had disappeared.

He forced himself to pick up one of the shrimp and dipped it into the sauce. No use letting good seafood go to waste. "Help yourself."

"Thanks." Nathan glanced at the door. "But I'm not very hungry."

"Let's wait a couple more minutes and call again.

You know how these mountains can interfere with reception."

Three minutes later and there was still no sign of the women. Nathan picked up his cell phone. "I'll try again."

Max watched as Nathan's jaw tensed.

"No answer?" Max asked after he'd flipped the phone shut.

"Trisha always carries her phone with her."

Max ran his fork through the butter sauce. "Think we should worry?"

"I don't know how not to. Logic tells me they're drinking tea with Riley and talking about bridesmaid gowns and wedding appetizers. Then on the other hand, there's the fact that there's two people dead and a murderer on the loose."

"Well, when you put it that way. . ."

Max bit his lower lip. He'd been determined not to let the weekend's events turn him into a worrywart. Of course, the last time Pricilla and his daughter had gone missing, they'd shown up soaking wet with a knife in their hands. And that didn't even begin to include things that had happened in the past with Pricilla. The woman was a magnet for trouble.

Nathan nodded. "I think we should find the sheriff."

Max pushed out his chair and stood. At the same moment, Sarah approached their table. "Mr. Summers? I'm sorry to interrupt your dinner."

Max looked down at the young woman. "No, that's fine. How are you?"

"I'm okay. . .well, no. I'm really not okay."

"Do you want to sit down?"

"I thought you were both leaving."

"We were, but if there's a problem. . ." Max sat back down.

She pressed her hand against her chest and sat down beside him. "Have you seen Michelle? I can't find her anywhere, and all the contestants and judges are supposed to be ready in the Great Room by six thirty. Michelle's never late. For anything."

Max glanced at his watch. "Did she leave the hotel?"

"She told me she needed to rush into town for something and would be right back. I offered to go, but she said it was something personal." Sarah gripped the wooden handle of her wicker bag. "I suppose I'm over-reacting, but with all that's happened this weekend. . . let's just say that while Michelle can be a tyrant to work for, I still don't want anything to happen to her."

"Is the sheriff around?" Max asked.

Sarah covered her mouth with her hand. "You don't think something's happened—"

"No, Sarah. I'm sure Michelle's fine," Max scrambled to reassure her. "She probably just got held up or had a flat tire or something."

"Like Pricilla and Trisha?" Nathan threw out.

Sarah's eyes widened. "What's happened to them?"

"They're missing as well," Nathan said.

Max pushed out his chair. "Listen, I'm sure we're all overreacting. I say we go to the Great Room. They're probably all there right now."

At least he hoped so. The only thing Max did know at the moment was that Trisha and Pricilla were missing, along with the person he considered to be the top suspect in a murder investigation.

Max tried not to panic as he quickly paid the bill and hurried behind Nathan toward the Great Room. Already the staff was busy preparing for the final ceremony that would be the culmination of the weekend. And with a quarter of a million dollars at stake, Max was certain that the evening would be spectacular. But at the moment, none of it interested him. What he needed now was to find either Pricilla and Trisha. . .or the sheriff.

Sheriff Lewis stood in the back of the room, leaning against the wall, a serious expression written on his face.

"Sheriff Lewis. I. . ." Max stopped in front of the lawman, then hesitated. Was he panicking for nothing?

"Anything wrong, Mr. Summers?"

"Pricilla's missing. . .again."

"And Trisha," piped in Nathan.

"And Michelle," Sarah added.

The lines on the sheriff's forehead seemed to multiply. The man looked tired. "Well, this is exactly what I need. Along with a string of murders, I now have an epidemic of missing people."

All doubts vanished from Max's mind. No. Something was definitely wrong. Three grown people couldn't just disappear.

The sheriff threw up his hands. "Start at the beginning. Where did Pricilla and Trisha go?"

"They left for town about four thirty to pick up Trisha's wedding dress," Nathan explained. "We were supposed to meet them for dinner about forty-five minutes ago."

"Where was Trisha's wedding dress?"

"At the house of a local seamstress. I think her name is. . .Riley?" Nathan looked to Max.

"Riley Michaels," Max finished.

"And what about Michelle?" the sheriff asked Sarah. "Where is she? With barely an hour left until the show begins, I would think the woman would be here pacing a hole in the carpet."

"So would I. And that's why I'm worried. All she told me was that she was going into town and that she'd be back in plenty of time." Sarah's forehead creased. "And as I told Nathan and Max, Michelle's never late."

Max felt his blood pressure rise. Never late until they were facing two murders, a murderer on the loose, and three missing people. He glanced at his watch and tried to convince himself that Pricilla had lost track of time, that the cell phone towers were down, and that she was, right now, having tea with Riley.

Except Pricilla would never skip a professional obligation for a cup of tea. Something was wrong.

The sheriff pulled out his cell phone. "There's still forty-five minutes until the show starts. I'm not sure this is the time to panic."

"All participants are required to be here early, which means Michelle would—"

"Okay." The sheriff held up his hand for Sarah to stop. "I see your point, but I can't exactly send out a search party without at least narrowing down the parameters. It will be dark before long, so anything you can tell me will help."

"I'd start between here and town," Max suggested. "It seems the most obvious."

"What about Miss Michaels?" the sheriff asked Sarah. "Have you talked to her?"

"I'll call information and try to get ahold of her now." Nathan stepped back from the group while the sheriff put in a call to the station.

A moment later, Nathan snapped his phone shut.

"Riley said they left at least thirty minutes ago."

"Thirty minutes ago?" Max questioned. "Town's not even ten minutes away."

"Where were they headed?" the sheriff asked.

"Back here, she said. Pricilla said something about not being late for the awards ceremony."

The sheriff shoved his hat on. "Then they should be somewhere between here and town. It's probably nothing more than a flat tire or dead battery."

Sarah didn't look convinced, and Max had to agree. "Both cars? It doesn't seem likely, sir."

She was right. What were the odds that both cars had broken down on the way back from town? It simply didn't make sense. If anyone wanted to put a stop to tonight's show, taking out both Michelle and Pricilla was a sure way. And if. . .Max shook his head and tried to rein in his wandering thoughts. Worrying only made things worse.

"So what are we waiting for?" Nathan fished his keys from his pocket. "Let's go."

A minute later, Max slid into the passenger seat of Nathan's car, praying that they would find the women. Quickly. The chance to spend the remaining years of his life with Pricilla had been a gift from God. He wasn't ready to lose her.

"This whole weekend has been a disaster." Nathan peeled out of the gravel driveway of the lodge, the worry evident on his face.

Max tried to think of something positive to momentarily offset his apprehension. "It hasn't been a complete disaster. Your mother and I managed to set a wedding date. Or at least narrow it down to a month. Which for us is progress."

"If I'd have known that a wedding was so complicated,

I'd have convinced Trisha to elope."

"The thought has crossed my mind a time or two."

"Why is it that women have turned weddings into something rivaling the Academy Awards, with all the fancy clothes and food to serve an army? The money for flowers and decorations alone would be better off invested in a college fund for future children."

Max chuckled but kept his gaze on the road for a sign of Pricilla's car. In another thirty minutes or so, the sun would set, making it harder to find them. "I don't know. When I married my first wife, which seems like forever ago now, things were different. All you needed was your friends and family, a homemade cake, and the local preacher."

Nathan flipped down the visor to block the setting sun. "Think Trisha might go for that?"

"I'd say it's far too late for homemade cake and a guest list under twenty-five."

For a moment, they were both quiet, lost in their own thoughts. *If something had happened to them. . .No.* Max reined in his thoughts. "They're going to be fine, Nathan."

"You can't know that."

"No, I can't."

Max gripped the armrest and started praying out loud. For Trisha and Pricilla. For Michelle. For the upcoming weddings. Clarissa. . .and the murderer. A chill that ran up his spine as he said "amen" was followed by a strange measure of peace.

"Thanks," Nathan said. "I guess I should have prayed before I started panicking."

"You and me both. I don't know why we think we can

rely on our own know-how until things are completely out of our control, but that seems to be the time that we normally send out the SOS."

Please, Lord. We're trusting You to help us find them.

Max searched the road ahead for any signs of a breakdown or a car that had gone off into the ditch. So far, nothing seemed out of place. They came to the T-junction and took a left toward town. If they hurried, there should still be enough light for them to search the other direction if they couldn't find them before getting into town.

"You know how much I love your daughter."

Max glanced at his future son-in-law. "Yes, I do."

"If anything were to happen to her. . .or to my mother. . ."

"Remember what I said earlier. It's far too early to give up."

Nathan tossed him his phone. "We're halfway to town. Why don't you try and call Trisha again. The reception's got to be better soon."

Max adjusted his bifocals and peered straight ahead. "Wait a minute."

"What is it?"

Max leaned forward, his heart stuck in his throat. "It's Pricilla's car."

They'd been kidnapped. Or so Pricilla was convinced. Why else would Michelle drive off with them, away from the lodge, while rambling on and on about who murdered Norton Richards? She glanced again at her watch for the umpteenth time, unable to brush aside the question. Even if Michelle wasn't the murderer, planning to add another two victims to her rampage, something was still wrong. With the awards ceremony starting in just over thirty minutes, there was a good chance they weren't going to make it back in time. Which meant that Michelle, who seemed to personify professionalism, had found something more pressing than the fulfillment of her contract and was now risking her career for it.

Pricilla studied the unfamiliar territory with its thick rows of pine trees. "We're going to be late."

"Don't worry about that right now." Michelle slowed down as she turned off onto another narrow dirt road. "We're almost there."

Trisha leaned forward and rested her chin on the red leather between the seats. "Almost where?"

"You told me you wanted to know if I killed Norton or not?" Michelle turned on the headlights.

"Well, yes, but—"

"Then that's exactly what you're going to know."

Pricilla worked to regulate her breathing. "Michelle, I think it's time you told us exactly what is going on."

"Like are you planning to murder us?" Trisha squeaked.

"Murder you?" Michelle's high-pitched laugh was far from reassuring. "Of course not. I'm planning to clear my name from your suspect list."

"Oh." Pricilla studied the open field nestled at the base of the mountain and frowned. "Then to be honest with you, Michelle, if your intention is to clear your name, at the moment you're not doing a very good job."

"Then I'm going to have to ask you to trust me."

Trust her? Right. Pricilla tightened her grip on the

armrest, still unsure where they were going as Michelle accelerated down the dirt road. As far as she was concerned, Michelle was either the murderer as she'd feared, or. . .or completely nuts.

"Max is going to think something has happened—"

"Mrs. Crumb, all I want is for you to believe that I'm more than a career woman on the fast track who would do anything to get what I want. Like murder."

They were all silent for a moment while Pricilla silently prayed that Michelle was telling the truth.

A small cabin sat fifty feet ahead. Michelle parked the car in front of it and shut off the engine but made no move to get out of the car. "When I was five, I remember watching the evening news with my father. I was mesmerized by how the newscaster was dressed, the way he talked, and the stories he recounted for the audience. They were full of drama and sadness and sometimes laughter. From that moment on, I wanted to do that. Find stories that made a difference in the lives of people. Except. . . except somewhere along the way, with the competition and rush of getting ahead, I realized that I'd lost that drive to discover the truth."

"I think we've all done that before," Pricilla said. "Forgotten why we're doing what we're doing."

"Like I forgot about the girl who had a dream to make it big in newscasting."

The truth hit Pricilla hard. *The Lord doesn't see things the way you see them. People judge by outward appearances, but the Lord looks at the heart.* For the first time, Pricilla began to see the woman sitting beside her in a different light. Young, vulnerable, full of ambition and hope. . .

The sun teetered on the edge of the mountain and

then fell behind it, leaving the valley in a hazy golden dusk.

"So what do you want to show us?"

"Have you ever heard the story about Millie Parks, the librarian who was found dead ten years ago on the bank of Lake Paytah wearing a purple scuba diving suit?" Michelle asked.

Pricilla's brow furrowed. "Yes. That was right in our neck of the woods. Far as I know the case was never solved."

"That's right. Well, Millie Parks had this fascination of history, perfect for a librarian. But she also had this strong sense of moral obligation. Unfortunately, it was this very passion that got her killed in the end."

"I don't understand."

"I've finally found my chance to prove I can do more than just host a cooking show or write an article about a bunch of food recipes."

"There's nothing wrong with that," Pricilla stated.

"Maybe not, but I still want more."

"What does Millie Parks have to do with any of this?" Trisha asked.

"I know who killed her."

Pricilla swallowed hard. "You know who killed her?"

"Fifteen or so years ago, a man by the name of Caleb Fountain bought ten thousand acres of land that included Lake Paytah."

"And he is somehow responsible for Millie's death?"

"Yes. The man I met with at the pharmacy is Millie's son. He's been trying to find out who killed her for the past ten years, but he's never been able to prove anything. Nor have the police."

"So how does this all connect with your big story?"

"What would happen if I told you that I've stumbled onto something that could actually make headline news on CNN?"

"Sounds like something huge."

"It is. You see, ten years ago Millie accidently stumbled onto something big that ended up costing her her life."

"What was it?" Pricilla asked.

"It has to do with Caleb Fountain and his land." Michelle opened her car door. "But first, I want you both to meet someone."

Pricilla moved to follow suit but then stopped. Someone had stepped out from the cabin. It was the man from the pharmacy.

He stood on the front porch, his arms folded across his chest, and frowned. "Michelle, what are you doing here?"

"I need you to meet someone, Greg."

"Michelle—"

"Mrs. Crumb, Trisha," Michelle began, interrupting the man. The three of them made their way toward the cabin. "I'd like you to meet Greg Parks."

Pricilla held out her hand, still not certain as to what was going on. "It's nice to meet you, Mr. Parks."

"You can call me Greg." The man's expression softened slightly, but he still wasn't smiling.

"All right, Greg."

Michelle swung her purse across her shoulder. "I need you to answer some questions for Mrs. Crumb."

"This isn't how we planned—"

"Please. You know I didn't want to involve you in any of this, but I'm a suspect in that murder case I told you about, and I'm not going to prison for something I didn't do." Michelle dipped her head toward Pricilla. "You can trust them."

Greg rubbed his goatee. "I don't know."

"Please, Greg."

He shrugged a shoulder. "I suppose it doesn't really matter at this point, does it? By tomorrow the whole country's going to know."

"Know what?" Pricilla pressed.

"You didn't tell her?"

"Of course not. But now. . ."

Trisha shivered beside Pricilla. "What's going on, Michelle?"

"He's my alibi, Mrs. Crumb. The one person who can prove I didn't kill Norton."

"If you have an alibi, then why all the secrets?"

"It's. . .complicated."

"Okay." Pricilla decided to leave it at that for now and forge ahead, even though she was still at a loss as to what was going on. "Were you with Michelle Wednesday night?"

The man nodded. "We met in town at Gardner's Bar about. . .ten o'clock I'd say."

"Why so late?"

He cocked his head toward Michelle. "She had a lot of work to do with the contest and couldn't get out until then."

"How long were you there?"

"They close at midnight. The owner locked the door behind us."

"You're certain it was midnight?"

"Positive. Frank Gardner's a stickler for closing on

time. You can ask anyone. He's too cheap to pay his workers any overtime."

"Then I drove directly to the lodge," Michelle continued. "I had just walked into the hotel when the sprinklers went off."

Pricilla quickly calculated the times. She'd glanced at the clock in her room right before she saw the two figures struggling in the darkness. It had been five minutes after midnight. If Michelle had left when the bar had closed, she would have indeed arrived just in time for the sprinklers to have gone off.

Pricilla cleared her throat, wishing the sheriff were here. "And you'll vouch for her whereabouts to the authorities?"

"Of course I will, though you're not exactly the authorities."

"No, but I'm certain that the sheriff will want to talk to you at some point."

"Are you satisfied now, Mrs. Crumb, that I'm innocent?" Michelle asked.

"I'm not the one you need to convince, but, yes, I am. What I don't understand is why you didn't tell this to the sheriff in the first place."

Michelle glanced at Greg. "We couldn't take a chance. As soon as things are over tonight, I'm going to break the story to the media."

"What story?" Pricilla asked.

"You'll have to watch tomorrow's news for the answer to that."

"So this is your big break as a reporter?"

Michelle actually smiled. "Yeah. You could say that."

"But why bring us here?" Trisha asked.

"Because I'm tired of the rumors and accusations. And, I suppose, of always being the bad guy."

"I guess we've all been guilty of judging you. I'm sorry," Pricilla admitted. "I do have one more question. You still haven't told us the reason for the clandestine meetings between the two of you."

Greg shook his head. "I said I'd vouch for you. I didn't promise anything else."

Michelle hesitated. "It's okay, Greg. They won't tell anyone. Will you?"

"Tell anyone what?" Trisha asked.

"I told you about the man who owns most of this land around here. Greg has been working undercover in his jelly lab where they make Temazepam."

"Temazepam?" Trisha asked. "What's that?"

"It's an illegal drug that's in high demand internationally." She nodded at Greg. "He can explain better than I can."

Greg sighed. "Temazepam is a hypnotic drug that ranks as one of the top-abused drugs in the world. In the past, most of the labs have been located throughout eastern Europe, but Mr. Fountain decided he wanted to try his hand at bringing in a little extra cash and set up his own indoor lab where he manufactures the drug."

"A little cash?"

"So that's a bit of an understatement. It's a billion-dollar industry for those who choose to get involved."

"I want this man shut down, Mrs. Crumb." Michelle's gaze dropped. "Three years ago, my brother died from a drug overdose."

"So this story is personal."

"It will make a difference to hundreds if this man is stopped. And I'm hoping for a CNN headline as well."

"And that's not all," Greg said. "Fountain killed my mother."

"I thought she drowned."

"No one scuba dives in Lake Paytah. They killed her because she was going to go to the authorities with information about his labs. The purple diving suit was either someone's idea of a sick joke or some crazy stunt to try and throw off the police."

"And you can prove all this?"

He nodded toward the house. "I managed to get the rest of what I needed today."

"So you're planning to break this story tomorrow."

"I came to Michelle because we're old friends, and I wanted a reporter I could trust with the news."

Michelle glanced at her watch. "For now, we'd better hurry back to the lodge. Sarah's probably in a tizzy, but we'll make it."

Pricilla started for the car, still trying to digest what Michelle had just told her.

"Thanks, Greg." Michelle followed them to the car. "Do you believe me, Mrs. Crumb?"

"Yes. Yes, I do."

Michelle pulled a U-turn and headed back toward the main road. She'd been telling the truth when she told Michelle she believed her, but now there was another problem. If Michelle hadn't had anything to do with Norton's death, then who had? Maybe she'd narrowed the field too much, as there still were all the ticket-holding audience members, and any of them could have had a vendetta against Norton. But if—

The blaring of sirens interrupted Pricilla's train of thought. She turned around to look as Trisha spoke.

"Mom. . ." Trisha started from the backseat.

Four police cars with flashing lights were blaring down the road behind them.

"I think you'd better pull over, Michelle."

They stepped from the car. Half a dozen officers had come out of their vehicles, their guns aimed directly at the three of them.

19

There she is!" Max jumped from the car and started running toward Pricilla.

"Wait." The sheriff grasped him by the forearm. "Until we know what's going on, I want the three of you standing right here behind the car. We don't need what could be a hostage situation going bad."

"A hostage situation. You can't be serious." Max felt his heart about to explode. How in the world had their relaxing weekend turned from sampling fresh prawns and asparagus to murder and kidnapping?

"After two murders and a few rounds of sabotage, I'm deadly serious."

Pricilla stepped out from the front of the red convertible and approached them slowly. Max adjusted his bifocals. Her face was pale, but otherwise she looked fine.

"Mrs. Crumb, are you all right?"

"Yes, I'm fine."

The sheriff moved in front of his vehicle. "Miss Vanderbilt, I want you to put your hands in the air where I can see them."

"Michelle's not the murderer, Sheriff," Pricilla called out.

Ignoring the lawman's order, Max took a step forward. Pricilla's life was at stake here, and he wasn't willing to stand back and do nothing. A bit like Pricilla, he supposed. "Are you really all right?"

Pricilla nodded. "I'm fine. This has all been a huge. . . a huge misunderstanding."

"What about the fact that you went missing with the number-one suspect of a murder investigation?" Max asked.

Pricilla looked to Michelle. "She decided she needed to prove to me that she's innocent."

"Innocent? And you actually believe her?" Max countered.

"Yes, I do. This whole. . .stunt. . .was because she wanted to show me the truth. She has an alibi for the night Norton was killed."

"And what is your alibi, Miss Vanderbilt?"

"A very long story," Pricilla jumped in. "And one all of us will know very soon."

The sheriff shook his head. "I don't understand."

"I'll make a deal with you, Sheriff Lewis." Pricilla glanced at her watch. "We've got exactly fifteen minutes to get back to the lodge for the awards ceremony. After it's over, I'll explain everything."

Red veins bulged in the sheriff's neck. "And you actually think I'm going to let the show continue after all of this."

"I think you should."

"Give me one good reason. There's a murderer on the loose, and I'm still not convinced that there isn't something strange going on here—"

"Those contestants have worked hard to prepare for this day. Michelle's worked hard. They deserve this opportunity."

"But—"

"Think of it as a chance to have all the suspects together one last time. At least you'll know where they all are."

"I don't know."

Michelle stepped forward. "Please, Sheriff Lewis. I realize that I haven't always been completely forthright with you, but I really can explain. There have been. . . extenuating circumstances."

"Is this a confession?"

"Only that I was wrong in not telling you the complete truth. But that aside, Mrs. Crumb is right. The winner deserves a moment in the spotlight and the television audience deserves to see who wins."

"What about you?" The sheriff obviously wasn't finished yet. "I'm sure you could use the limelight as well."

Michelle lowered her hands. "I didn't kill Norton or Freddie, but I can promise you that after the show is over, I'll tell you everything."

"You're certain about this, Mrs. Crumb?"

Pricilla nodded.

"Okay. Then I expect to see all of you back at the lodge in five minutes. Looks like somebody's got a show to put on."

Pricilla slid into the backseat of Nathan's car and slouched against the leather interior. "I can't believe I have to cross my number-one suspect from my list. Number two is dead, and there isn't enough evidence against anyone else to make a solid case."

Nathan started the engine and headed toward the lodge behind the sheriff. "You should be glad your field is narrowing."

"Narrowing? That's the problem. It isn't. Not really. But for the moment, I have more pressing things to deal with."

"For instance?"

"Those cameras are about to roll, and I look—"

"Beautiful." Max reached out to squeeze her hand. "As far as I'm concerned, you always do."

"You know I don't deserve you." Pricilla fished in her purse for a tube of lipstick. She pulled out a pair of sunglasses, her powder compact, and the stack of papers Max had printed out for her.

"You never told me if any of that information helped."

"It became my late-night reading." Pricilla glanced at the stapled pile. "Honestly, though, I think it only made more questions by adding to the motives of most of the suspects."

Trisha sat snuggled up with Nathan in the front seat. "What are they?"

"Pages Max downloaded from the Internet the other day."

"I figured the sooner the investigation was closed, the sooner Pricilla would be back to. . .back to being Pricilla," Max admitted.

"You wouldn't want me any other way now, would you?"

Max chuckled as the truth hit home. "Holmes and Watson always did make a good team."

"And they always managed to solve the case. Something we haven't been able to do."

"At least you were able to cross one suspect from your list," Max said. "And speaking of Michelle, did you notice her photo?"

"Several of them gave me a good laugh, to be honest. Look at this picture of Michelle." Pricilla handed the page to Trisha.

"She's obviously lost all her small-town image," Trisha said.

Pricilla passed a second page. "And Freddie. I'd never recognize him. The man must have had some plastic surgery to have those ears pinned back."

"Wow. You're right. You'd never recognize him, would you? Seventy-five pounds lighter at least, short hair, no glasses."

Pricilla froze at the description. "Trisha?"

"What is it?"

"Can I have that page of Freddie again, please?"

Trisha handed the page back to Pricilla. "What is it?"

Pricilla sucked in her breath. Everything clicked.

"I can't believe I didn't see this. I knew I'd seen him somewhere before. It all makes sense now."

"I don't understand," Max said. "What are you talking about?"

"The killer. We've been on the wrong trail this entire time." Pricilla leaned forward and tapped Nathan on the shoulder. "Flash your lights at the sheriff. I've got to speak with him immediately."

"What?"

"Please, Nathan. Flash your lights. I need him to stop."

Nathan flashed his lights and started to slow down. "Would you please tell us what's going on?"

"I know who killed Norton. . .and Freddie."

———

Pricilla had obviously been wrong. She scanned the audience and tried to calm the butterflies knotting up in her stomach. To the left, the judges sat at their private table. Max, Nathan, and Trisha sat near the front, looking as anxious as she felt. They were already twenty minutes into the evening's ceremony, and so far, everything had gone without a hitch. The sheriff's deputies were in the process of searching the grounds, but from her perch in the front of the Great Room, her plan hadn't worked. There had been little time to explain her suspicions to the sheriff. Even Max had been left in the dark as she'd flagged down the sheriff and driven with him back to the lodge. But the bottom line was that the murderer hadn't shown up for the grand finale as she'd anticipated.

The red light came on and Pricilla forced a smile. "Ladies and gentlemen, it's been a privilege to be a part of this weekend's Fifteenth Annual Rocky Mountain Chef Competition. This evening is the culmination of three days of activities, and *Food Style* magazine is now prepared to award the quarter of a million dollars to the winner of this year's competition. So now for the moment we've all been waiting for. The winner of this year's competition is. . ." Pricilla took the black envelope from Michelle and started to open it.

A streak of yellow crackled along the edge of the room and caught her eye. Someone screamed. The curtains lining the large windows burst into flames. Someone shouted. The fire alarm went off, followed by the sprinkler system.

A shower of water sprayed on Pricilla. She felt her knees go weak as the soggy envelope slipped from her fingers.

The sheriff quickly took charge, shouting above the noise. "I want everyone to leave the building through the south exit in an orderly fashion. No running. No panicking. Everything's under control."

Trying to catch a glimpse of her suspect, Pricilla

watched as the audience scurried from the room. She was still standing in front of the camera when Max appeared beside her. "We've got to go!"

"I can't leave. Not yet." A drip of water splashed off the end of her nose. Between the sprinklers and a fire extinguisher, the fire seemed to be out, but if they didn't catch the murderer in the act. . .

"Come on, Pricilla."

She nodded and followed him out the door. There was nothing else she could do here.

The sheriff met her outside the building, soaked like the rest of them. "We did it!"

Her eyes widened. "We did?"

The sheriff wiped his chin with the back of his hand. "Not only is the sprinkler system working, but it seems as if you were right, Mrs. Crumb."

The sheriff was smiling for the first time all weekend as one of the deputies walked toward them, gripping Riley Michaels's arm.

Pricilla caught the young woman's fiery gaze and felt a ping of guilt. "I didn't want to be right."

"One of my deputies caught her with a box of gasoline-soaked rags. She managed to set the curtains on fire by using a fuse, but that's as far as she got." The sheriff turned to Pricilla. "If you hadn't told us who to look for, we might have had a real disaster on our hands right now."

"Riley?" Trish slid in between Pricilla and Max. "I don't understand. . . . I thought. . ."

Riley tried to jerk away from the officer's grip. "I didn't do anything. This is nothing more than a big mistake, like the arrest of. . .of Clarissa. I was just. . ."

"Just what, Miss Michaels?" the sheriff asked.

Pricilla shivered in the cool breeze and pulled her sweater tighter around her shoulders. Part of her still wished she'd been wrong, but the smell of gasoline on the girl was all the additional proof Pricilla needed. "I never would have believed it, if I hadn't seen the pieces laid out before me like some crazy jigsaw puzzle."

The sheriff took a garbled call on his radio and then turned to Riley. "We lucked out and caught the judge at home, and thankfully, he was willing to grant us a search warrant."

"And. . ." Pricilla prodded.

"And one of my deputies just found the murder weapon in Riley's house. A pair of eight-inch sewing shears."

"You have no right to search my house—"

"No right? You should have thought of that before you decided to kill a man. Two men, actually. And then tried to burn down the lodge."

"I didn't plan to kill Norton." Her voice was lathered with anger. "He. . .my parents lost their business because of him. He deserved anything he got."

The sheriff shook his head. "I found out this evening that The Krab Kettle went out of business because your father was dipping into the till to feed his gambling habit, and your parents went bankrupt."

"None of it would have happened without that review he posted of the restaurant." Riley's expression was one of a trapped animal. "That restaurant meant everything to my parents. They worked for years to build up their clientele until Norton ruined it all with one stroke of his deadly pen and gave them a two-star rating. When I found out he was coming. . ." She dipped her head. "All I planned to do was talk to him. . .and to tell him how he ruined my life."

"But you had your scissors with you. Sounds pretty premeditated to me," the sheriff told her. "And then there was Freddie."

"I never meant to hurt Freddie, but he. . .he wanted out."

"Out of blackmailing Lyle and sabotaging the kitchens in order to win the contest? I hardly blame him."

"The sabotaging was Freddie's idea." Riley's jaw tensed. "I'm not saying anything else until I have a lawyer."

"That's just fine, Miss Michaels. You've already said everything I needed to hear. Take her away, deputy."

Riley started crying. "You don't understand. I needed the money. Freddie promised me he could win. And if I wasn't going to get the money. . ."

Max shook his head as they led Riley toward the squad car. "Now that this is all over, do you think you might explain, Sheriff? I have to admit I'm still a bit confused as to exactly what tipped you off."

"Would you like to do the honors, Mrs. Crumb?"

Pricilla smiled at her captive audience. She'd liked Riley and hated that she'd been the one they were looking for, but her arrest also meant that all charges against Clarissa would be dropped.

"There were several clues that on their own didn't mean anything," Pricilla began. "But I started to wonder if we hadn't been looking in the wrong place. First of all, I knew Norton had reviewed Riley's parents' restaurant, which was my first connection with Norton. Then there was the overnight express package I'd seen from Sally's Scissors Emporium on Riley's veranda table. Why would

Riley suddenly need a new pair of scissors?"

"Because she'd used hers to kill Norton?" Max said.

"Exactly. She had them overnighted to replace the ones she stabbed him with. And then there was Freddie," Pricilla continued.

"Freddie?" Trisha asked.

"You remember the family photographs hanging up in Riley's hall. When I saw those printouts from Max the second time, I recognized that the rotund figure standing outside the restaurant beside Riley was Freddie—a hundred or so pounds heavier. Riley convinced Freddie they could rig the contest and win the quarter of a million dollars."

The sheriff nodded. "That's not all. Lyle Simpson admitted to us that Freddie had a photo of him and a woman who wasn't his wife. When they added a few acts of sabotage to blackmail, Freddie and Riley convinced themselves they were on the fast track to winning the prize money. Clarissa's arrest worked right into their plan. The young woman made the perfect fall guy. Riley even stole the knife from Clarissa's kitchen in hopes of further incriminating her."

"I'm sure she didn't plan for anyone to find the knife so quickly and prove it wasn't the murder weapon," Pricilla added. "But Trisha's lost ring messed up those plans. I'm sure Freddie's death was unplanned, but Riley couldn't have Freddie panicking and confessing what they'd done."

Pricilla turned to Trisha. "Even you and I played right into her hands. Riley knew I was helping out the sheriff so every dress fitting ended up giving her an inside look into what was happening with the case. And we never suspected a thing. Plus, it gave her access to the lodge without anyone questioning her presence.

"When Riley said she had something left to do tonight, I wondered if she had something else planned. As she just implied, if she couldn't get the money, then she didn't want anyone else to get it."

Another call came through for the sheriff.

"That was one of my deputies I sent over to Riley's house after we got a search warrant," he said. "They just found what we believe to be the murder weapon—a pair of shears."

"Wait a minute," Trisha began. "You just told Riley you'd already found them."

The sheriff smiled. "I decided to gamble. When Mrs. Crumb told me she suspected that Miss Michaels's shears were the murder weapon, and the coroner confirmed that they could be, I decided to try to get a confession out of her."

"It worked, but I have a question," said Pricilla. "Where were they? I saw her house today, and I can't imagine anyone finding them quickly."

"I've got a couple of smart deputies. They were hidden in the tank of her bedroom toilet."

"A bit of a cliché, don't you think?" Max said.

"It only goes to prove who's the amateur and. . ." The sheriff glanced at Pricilla. "Who's the professional."

Pricilla felt her cheeks blush in spite of the chilly breeze and her wet attire.

"I'd be privileged to work with you again anytime, Mrs. Crumb," he added.

"Thanks for the vote of confidence, Sheriff." She turned to Max. "But now that Clarissa's about to be released, I'd say we have a wedding to plan."

20

Pricilla entered the elegant dining room that was situated on the fourth floor, set up for Nathan and Trisha's rehearsal dinner. She took Max's proffered arm and glanced out the row of large picture windows. The twinkling lights of Denver began to emerge as the sun sank behind the lofty Rocky Mountains, making the perfect backdrop. The stylish table, set for twenty, was adorned with a white tablecloth and crystal candlesticks with gold candles. Already more than a dozen of Nathan and Trisha's friends were gathered around the table, ready for the appetizers to be served.

"Marriage isn't as easy today as it was when we were young, is it?" Max said.

"Nor, it seems, is the actual wedding. After all that's managed to go wrong with this one, I'm glad we're almost through with it."

"I have a feeling they'll make it."

Pricilla nodded, amazed at how God had brought them all together. Her son and his daughter, Max and her. . .

"You're late, Mom." Trisha and Nathan approached them from the other side of the room. Trisha's deep purple dress fell in soft folds around her waist and swirled to her ankles.

"Everything looks beautiful, Trisha."

Her son kissed her on the cheek. "And so do you. But I was getting worried."

Pricilla winked at him. "Worried I'd managed to get myself caught up in another murder mystery?"

"I admit I'm not quite as worried as I have been now that Riley's behind bars."

"You don't have to worry about me." She looked at Max and laughed. "I've decided to just read my mysteries and leave the investigations to capable people like Sheriff Lewis."

Nathan cleared his throat. "Now why do I have a hard time believing that? With your knack for finding trouble, there always seems to be plenty of it."

"Plenty of trouble? I'd say quite the opposite. Clarissa's record has been wiped clean, Michelle was offered a position as an anchor with a major network after her story broke, Christopher Jeffries is now studying in Paris, and Sarah landed a book contract that will allow her to hire her own girl Friday if she wants." Pricilla glanced at Max and smiled. "Besides, I've already found everything I need right here."

She felt her breath catch. There had always been something mesmerizing about his eyes that left her breathless. She might not have expected a second chance at love, but she'd be forever grateful to God for giving it to her.

"Mom?"

Pricilla turned back to their kids, forcing herself to focus. For tonight she was going to leave any daydreaming behind. Tonight was for Nathan and Trisha. "Sorry, I—"

"What is it with you two?" Trisha cocked her head. "You look positively. . .positively blissful."

Pricilla shook her head. This wasn't the way she wanted things to go. "This weekend is for the two of you, remember, and nothing's going to get in the way of that. Tonight's the rehearsal dinner, then tomorrow's the wedding ceremony at the church." She shot Max a dreamy look. "You haven't seen the church yet, but the eighteenth-century building has the most stunning stained-glass windows in the front. Then it's off to the Bahamas for your honeymoon—"

Nathan folded his arms across his chest and shot her that familiar look of his. She knew that look. She rambled when she got excited, and he clearly had no intention of letting her off the hook. "Mom, something's up. What is it?"

She attempted to dodge the subject. "Why do you assume that because I have a smile on my face something's up? And besides, you were right when you said we were late, which means it must be time we all sat down to eat. Right, Max? There's nothing more disparaging to your guests than to serve the appetizer lukewarm—"

"We've got to have the most exasperating parents alive." Trisha nudged Nathan. "I've just never seen the two of you look so. . .so glowing."

"And young," Nathan added.

"Yes." Trish nodded. "And young."

Glowing. Blissful. Young. Pricilla couldn't help but giggle. She could get used to descriptions like that. And while she knew the cream-colored suit and moisturizer she wore couldn't really erase the years, she did feel about twenty-five again tonight.

"Mom?"

"Dad?"

Max clasped her hand. "We might as well tell them."

Pricilla shrugged and then nodded. "I suppose it's the only way they'll let us sit down and eat. I don't know about you, but I'm starving."

"Me, too. I hear the food is great, but the servings

leave a bit to be desired—"

"Dad. What do you have to tell us?" Trisha threw out.

"Your father and I. . ." Pricilla began. "We eloped."

"You eloped? You didn't."

"We did."

"You eloped?" Nathan repeated.

"Yes, we did."

Trisha's shocked expression melted into a broad smile. "This is wonderful, but. . ."

"But what?"

"What about the church and the wedding gown and—I was looking forward to another wedding."

"But I, for one, didn't want the hassle of misspelled invitations, oversized wedding dresses, and—"

"And a seamstress who turns out to be a murderer," Trisha said.

"Exactly, and—"

"Hold on." Nathan laughed and pulled Trisha toward him. "I'd say we get the point."

Pricilla smiled. She'd meant it when she said she didn't need a fancy dress, dozens of guests, and piles of rich food as an essential backdrop to her proclaiming her love to Max. A wedding ring on her finger and a marriage certificate from the courts really was enough for her.

"All I've wanted all along was to be Mrs. Pricilla Summers. I don't need the hassles of a wedding ceremony for that."

Trisha scurried to the table and grabbed four of the crystal fluted water glasses. Ice chinked against the sides as she handed them out and then turned to the rest of the guests sitting at the long table. "If I could get your attention, everyone, I'd like to propose a toast to Max and Pricilla, who somehow managed to make it to the altar before we did." She held up her glass. "May you both enjoy years of love and laughter ahead of you. . .together."

"Hear, hear!"

"Bravo!"

"Congratulations!"

"Thank you." Pricilla felt the heat of a blush rush to her cheeks as she turned her face to Max.

He leaned down and brushed his lips across hers. "Whoever said that eloping was scandalous had no idea what they were talking about. Isn't that right, Mrs. Summers?"

Pricilla held up her glass and smiled. "That's exactly right, Mr. Summers."

Lisa Harris is a wife, mother, and author who has been writing both fiction and nonfiction for the Christian market since 2000. She and her husband, along with their three children, live in Mozambique where they are missionaries. Life is busy between ministry and homeschooling, but she cherishes the time she has to escape into another world and write. She sees this work as an extension of her ministry. For a glimpse into Lisa's life in Africa, visit mybloginheartofafrica.blogspot.com or visit her Web site at www.lisaharriswrites.com.

You may correspond with this author by writing:
Lisa Harris
Author Relations
PO Box 721
Uhrichsville, OH 44683

A Letter to Our Readers

Dear Reader:

In order to help us satisfy your quest for more great mystery stories, we would appreciate it if you would take a few minutes to respond to the following questions. We welcome your comments and read each form and letter we receive. When completed, please return to:

Fiction Editor
Heartsong Presents—MYSTERIES!
PO Box 721
Uhrichsville, Ohio 44683

Did you enjoy reading *Chef's Deadly Dish* by Lisa Harris?

Very much! I would like to see more books like this!
The one thing I particularly enjoyed about this story was:

_____

_____

_____

Moderately. I would have enjoyed it more if:

_____

_____

_____

Are you a member of the HP—MYSTERIES! Book Club?
Yes   No

If no, where did you purchase this book?

_____

Please rate the following elements using a scale of 1 (poor) to 10 (superior):

___ Main character/sleuth   ___ Romance elements

___ Inspirational theme   ___ Secondary characters

___ Setting   ___ Mystery plot

How would you rate the cover design on a scale of 1 (poor) to 5 (superior)? _____

What themes/settings would you like to see in future **Heartsong Presents—MYSTERIES!** selections? _____

_____

_____

_____

Please check your age range:
- ◯ Under 18   ◯ 18–24
- ◯ 25–34   ◯ 35–45
- ◯ 46–55   ◯ Over 55

Name: _____

Occupation: _____

Address: _____

E-mail address: _____